Heidi Cullinan

Dreamspinner Press

Published by
Dreamspinner Press
4760 Preston Road
Suite 244-149
Frisco, TX 75034
http://www.dreamspinnerpress.com/

Hero

Cover Art by Paul Richmond   http://www.paulrichmondstudio.com

ISBN: 978-1-61581-286-8

Printed in the United States of America
First Edition
December, 2009

eBook edition available
eBook ISBN: 978-1-61581-287-5

For Shelly B,
because most of the time I was writing it
I kept thinking, "Shelly is so going to love this."

And for my husband Dan,
because the first book published was
always going to be dedicated to him.

My belt holds my pants up, but the belt loops hold my belt up.
So which one's the real hero?

—Mitch Hedberg

ACKNOWLEDGMENTS

THE thank you section in a first sale book is always long, and this one is no exception because a great number of people have carried me to this moment.

Thanks go first to Corrina Lawson, because she was the one who suggested I try writing a male/male romance, and without that nudge this book would never have happened. Thanks also go to Brad Hanon, editor of *Syzygy Magazine*, who not only confirmed that I actually could write a pretty decent male/male romance but helped me make the one I wrote for him better and further encouraged me to try my hand at something longer.

Thanks go in great big buckets to my beta readers, J.L. Merrow, Kari Hayes, and Susan Danic, who told me what worked and what didn't. *Hero* wouldn't be half the book it is without your input, and I can't thank you enough.

Thanks go to the many, many writing communities that have supported me over the past eight years. All had a hand, in their own way, in helping me get to the point of writing acknowledgments for my first book: to the Whiners, the Cherries, the Glindas, to Captain Jack's Walrus, to my LiveJournal friends, and to the Central Iowa Authors (yea, crap!), I say thank you for your support, your wisdom, your kindness, and your love. I'm blessed to have so many communities, and I love you all.

Thanks go to my family, to Tom and Nina Cullinan, the in-laws who are always encouraging me, who have always believed I could do it, and who don't bat an eye at lending their surname to a gay romance. Thanks go to my daughter Anna for being patient with a mother who is always at the computer and for putting away her own laundry and making her own peanut butter sandwiches perhaps a little more than she should. I love you, Anna. Thanks for helping your mom so much.

But more than anyone else, thanks go to Dan Cullinan, my beautiful, wonderful partner. For years and years, you have done nothing but support my writing, never complaining when you came home from a long day of work to find me zoned out at the computer and the sink full of dishes with a pile of unwashed laundry on the side. For years you have sent me to conferences, bought me computers and books, sent me on trips, and turned a blind eye to far, far too many iTunes purchases for the never-finished writing playlist.

You have read every word I have written, usually before anyone else, and you have read draft after draft of each story, never once complaining that you've read it too many times. You have been my strength when I have had none, my confidence when I have run out. You have carried me through this when I have been sick, when I have been surly, and when I have been despondent. You have celebrated my joys and nursed my sorrows.

In short, you above all others have shown me what a true romantic hero should look like. There aren't words to thank someone for this kind of support and inspiration, but I hope these make something of a start. I love you, Dan, and I could not have done this without you.

Heidi Cullinan

December 2009

CHAPTER 1
The Disappearing Bar

HAL PORTER was just finishing up his shift for the day at the Santa Monica site, hauling tools back to the shed, when the building appeared out of nowhere.

It was in the lot adjacent to the construction site, in the patch of land that Hal would have sworn had been empty just that morning. Granted, it was only his second day working on this site, but Gerry, the foreman, had stood glaring at it as he chain-smoked furiously less than an hour ago, grousing about how some "hippie weirdo" owned it and wouldn't sell, how they had to work around that one damn lot, and what a bitch it was going to be. The police had their eyes on it too, apparently. People kept turning up dead in it. They suspected the deaths were gang-related, but it was a long way to go to dump a body. Rape victims woke up here, too, for some reason. It was a weird, creepy place, and Gerry had advised Hal to avoid it, especially if the shift ran late. And yet, as Hal stood there, he was not looking at an empty patch of ground, nothing but weeds and sand. He was looking at a building, three stories tall, looking like it had been there for over a hundred years.

A woman was standing in front of it.

1

She stood beneath the awning—a sagging, battered green and white striped overhang—and a dingy plastic sign that read, simply, "BAR." The woman, however, was not dingy or saggy. She was sleek and expensive: small, dark-haired, decked out in a pristine white dress and heels and, of all things, a thick fur coat. It was Los Angeles, and it was an eighty-eight degree day in July, and she was wearing a fur coat that would have kept her warm in Juneau, Alaska.

The woman was looking at Hal, her dark eyes full of suspicion, but after a few minutes she turned away from him and toward the building, studying it carefully. She paced up and down the sidewalk in front of it slowly, like a tiger, but aside from occasional glances at Hal, she didn't take her eyes off it. *Hungry,* Hal thought as he watched her. She looked hungry. It wasn't a hunger for food, either. She was hungry for... something. Shielding his eyes from the afternoon sun with his free hand, Hal stopped and stared, his eyes shifting from the woman to the building and back again. There was something she wanted. Desperately. Something in that building.

Something, a voice whispered in the back of his mind, *she's wanted for a long, long time.*

She turned toward Hal again, and this time their eyes met. She wasn't glaring any longer; in fact, she looked surprised. She took a step toward Hal, tentatively, and Hal waited, still watching. He began to feel strange, as if he were falling asleep with his eyes open. *Or maybe,* he thought, his head spinning, so light now that he had to hold back the urge to laugh, *I'm just now coming awake.* He didn't laugh, but he did smile, and when the woman saw this, she smiled back.

Then she lifted her hand and blew him a kiss.

Light flashed. It was a small flash, so subtle it could have been the sun reflecting off a mirror, but it came from her hand, and when the light hit Hal's eyes, he stepped forward. He dropped the tools he was holding and started toward the woman standing in front of the imaginary bar, the woman who was now beckoning to him. *I'm coming*, he thought, and he started walking faster. The sights and sounds of the construction site faded away, becoming blurs and distant *tink-tink-tinks* as the world narrowed to that woman, that building, and the space between them. *I'm coming.*

I'll go inside, he thought, his gaze shifting to the door of the bar. He could see it now, tall and dark—taller and darker than it had a right to be—but he knew, somehow, it didn't matter. He would open the door. Nothing could stop him from opening that door. *And when I'm inside, I'll find it. I'll find what she's looking for. What I'm looking for too.*

I'll find him. I'll find him, and I'll bring him home.

"Hey!"

The shout jarred in Hal's head, but it wasn't until something butted him hard in the elbow that he stopped. He turned, dizzy and annoyed, and then stifled a wince when he saw who it was. It was Todd, the shift manager. The other crew members had warned Hal about Todd—he didn't do much work, they said, because he was too busy watching everyone else. Some thought he was some sort of spy for the investors. Whatever he was, he was strange. Todd was short and stocky and had the complexion of a toad, but he had oddly bright blond hair that for some inexplicable reason he wore in a pageboy bob. The bob was gleaming at Hal now as Todd glared.

"What are you doing?" Todd demanded. "Aren't you supposed to be working?"

Hal looked at him strangely. "They just called end of shift ten minutes ago," he reminded Todd. *You were the one shouting through the megaphone. Remember?*

Todd glared and nodded at the bar, making his gleaming hair dance again. "Then why are you heading back into the site?"

"I'm not," Hal said, pointing to the bar. "I was just—" He stopped. Then he stared.

The woman was gone. The bar was gone. The lot was empty again.

"You were just what?" Todd demanded.

Hal ignored him. "I swear, I saw—" He leaned forward, squinting, as if somehow this would help. It didn't. He straightened up and ran a hand through his hair. "Nothing," he said, trying to sound casual. "I thought I saw something, but I didn't." He shook his head and then bent to retrieve the tools he'd dropped. "Forget it. I'm just tired. I'm seeing things."

"This heat will do it to you." Todd was watching Hal like a hawk. "You should go home. Get some sleep."

"Or get drunk," Hal murmured, and then he shouted and dropped the tools again when he looked up.

The bar was back, and so was the woman. She was looking at him with wide, angry eyes, and she was beckoning to him furiously.

"What is it now?" Todd demanded, but he didn't sound impatient. He sounded wary.

Hal rubbed at his head, pretty sure there was something wrong with it. He glanced at the shift manager. "That lot over there, the empty one—you see anything in it?" The woman shook her head and began to motion to him more frantically. Hal added, carefully, "You see any*body* standing there?"

Todd laughed. Nervously. "It's bed for you," he said. "Either that or you need to get laid."

4

Hal turned to Todd, frowning at him. "What do you mean, I need to get laid?"

Todd drew back. He looked suddenly strained and held up his hands. "Hey, it's you hallucinating women, buddy."

Hal raised his eyebrows. "I never said it was a woman that I saw."

Todd's complexion went from ruddy to pale. "You did. I remember." He took a few more hurried steps backward. "Hey, look, I gotta—" He turned abruptly and then waddled off toward the office trailer.

Hal watched him go, more confused than ever. So Todd *had* seen something. Hal wasn't hallucinating—or, at least, it wasn't just him hallucinating. But Todd was upset by it. Why? And what did it all mean?

The woman—and the bar—were still there. She was gesturing to him again, no longer angry, just desperate. Hal felt the pull, the strange, surreal longing to go to her, to go inside, to seek. He took a few steps toward her, hesitant, and he watched the world fade away again. He saw, this time, even the bar fade away, and for a moment, he could see inside.

He saw a man, slight and slim and beautiful, reaching down to him from a glass castle in the clouds.

Hal drew in a sharp breath. *No,* he thought, and he stepped back.

There was a loud crack, another flash of light, and then the building and the woman were gone. The lot was empty. The world was normal again.

For several minutes, Hal stood there, frowning, trying to figure it out. But nothing made sense, and in the end, he told himself he didn't care. Whatever was going on was none of his business. He didn't want to get in trouble, and if Todd wasn't a spy, he was at the very least a little strange. And so was this mystery woman who appeared and disappeared at will with a bar in an empty lot. He ignored them all and went toward the bus stop, heading for home.

But he couldn't shake the strange, empty feeling in the pit of his stomach that whispered, urgently, that he had just made a very big mistake.

THE nagging feeling faded by the time he made it back to Hollywood. On the way, he'd stopped at his post office box in Culver City and picked up his mail, which had included a package from his mother. It included, as it always did, a lengthy handwritten letter, a week's worth of *The Emporia Gazette*, a dozen peanut butter cookies, and a copy of the latest *Catholic Digest*. He nibbled at a few cookies as he perused the papers on the bus, and he read the letter while he heated a can of soup for dinner. Once he'd done the dishes, he sat down on his sofa, put the *Digest* on the footlocker he used for a coffee table, went back for a few more cookies, and then began to leaf through the magazine.

He didn't read a word, but occasionally he stopped turning pages and reached in to withdraw the dollar bills his mother had hidden inside. Most were ones, but there were a few fives, and as he found a pair of twenties around an article about the sanctity of marriage, he frowned. When he came to the last page, he started at the beginning again, double-checking. Once he was convinced he'd gleaned them all, he counted the stack, rose and crossed to the marker board hanging by the door, picked up the dry erase marker that hung on a string beside it, and wrote, carefully, "$67 extra to Mom."

Then he went back to the couch, pulled his cell phone out of his pocket, and dialed a number.

"Howard, I was just thinking of you," his mother said when she answered. "That nice Janice Holford was just here to drop off some Avon. She asked about you—how were you doing in the big city, and if you were coming home sometime this summer." There was excitement in her voice as she added, "She's still single, you know."

"I just got your package," Hal said, deflecting. "Thank you very much."

"Did the cookies make it?" she asked. She always asked.

She also always cased them in enough bubble wrap to ship a raw egg. "Tasted like they just came out of the oven," Hal assured her.

"Oh good. I'll send some more next week, so don't be shy about eating them up. Has work been going well?"

"A lot of overtime." Hal leaned back into the couch. He thought about the hallucinations and thought to himself, *Maybe too much.* "I'm going to send you another check, Mom, and don't put it all into your savings again. Go buy yourself something nice." *And stop putting money in the* Catholic Digest.

"Sweetheart, you work too hard," she scolded. "You need a vacation. When are you going to come back home?"

"When are you going to come to Los Angeles?" he countered.

"Oh Howard! I could never."

"You could," he pointed out, "if you quit letting the airfare vouchers I send you expire. You'd like it here more than you think, Mom."

This was not exactly true—she would hate Hollywood, which was where Hal currently lived. But he always had his eye out for decent housing in a better area, and he figured about the time he found something he could afford would be when his mom would actually get on a plane.

That would also be around the time he actually read the *Catholic Digest*.

"I just wish you'd come home," his mother said sadly. "All you do there is work. You could do that here. We still have construction in Kansas."

"Better opportunity here," he replied, but weakly—it wasn't exactly true anymore. He'd come here hoping to get some good experience and work his way up the ladder, certain that the good-old-boy network that had frustrated him in Kansas wouldn't be as impervious in such a large city. But it turned out that the only difference between Los Angeles, California, and Emporia, Kansas, was that Los Angeles was bigger and had an ocean next to it. If anything, the ceiling of success here was even thicker and higher above his head. And now there was Todd, the company spy.

"You work too hard," his mother said again. "And they don't pay you enough. I Googled that apartment complex you live in. It isn't safe."

Hal thought of the gunshots he'd heard the night before and had to agree, though he did so privately. "Soon, Mom," he promised. "Things will break soon." He thought of the disappearing woman and bar and hoped that it wouldn't be his mind that broke. He reached up to his neck, fingered the necklace that hung there, and sighed. "I'll come home before the year is out," he promised. "But once I do, then you have to come here."

"I don't like airplanes," his mother said. "And I can't drive in that place."

"Then I'll drive you," Hal said, but that was an empty promise until he had a car that would make the three-thousand-mile round-trip.

"I just want to see you happy," his mom said with a sad sigh. "That's all I've ever wanted, Hal. And you're not happy there, I can tell."

"I wasn't happy in Emporia," he reminded her.

"You won't be happy anywhere," she said, "until you start believing in yourself. You can do anything you put your mind to, Howard. You're a smart, capable, handsome man who would be an asset to any job and a good husband to whomever you chose to spend your life with."

Hal grimaced and stared down at the magazine lying open on the footlocker. It had turned itself to the marriage article again, where a wholesome, happy woman in white was sailing down the steps of a cathedral, cherub-like girls with flower crowns at her feet and a clean-shaven, handsome man in a black tuxedo looking fondly over her shoulder. You could almost see the suburban house and shiny SUV reflected in her eyes, and the board meeting in her husband's. Hal glowered at them both and shut the magazine.

"How's Aunt Lottie doing?" he asked.

"Oh, you know her," his mother said bitterly and then launched into a recitation of all the wild and strange things his maiden aunt had done in the past seven days. Hal shut his eyes and leaned back into the cushions, letting the words wash over him. But he kept seeing the bride and her husband in his mind's eye, and when he pushed them aside, he saw the vanishing woman from the lot again.

When he finally got off the phone, he flipped through the channels on the television, but nothing caught his interest. By nine he gave up, showered, and went to bed. He set his alarm on his phone and plugged it into the wall, laid out his clothes, pulled off his towel, and climbed into bed.

He lay there on the sheets for a long time, hands behind his neck as he stared up at the ceiling.

He couldn't stop thinking about that bar or the way he'd felt when he looked at it. The woman unsettled him, but the bar had been... hypnotizing. Every time he shut his eyes, he saw it, and in his state of half-sleep, half-waking, he kept seeing the figure inside. He kept waking himself up, so he couldn't make out who it was, but every time the shadow appeared, he ached for it. And if he slipped deep enough into the trance, he felt it coming closer.

Once, he'd seen the eyes, and they burned into the back of his brain. And when he stared into those eyes, other parts of his body burned too.

At ten-thirty, Hal sat up. He turned on his bedside light and reached into a drawer, digging beneath the old *Emporia Gazettes* that had made their way between the editions of *Time* his mother sometimes sent, fumbling for the thin, brown paper bag at the bottom. He pulled out the magazine inside, rolling his eyes at himself for his flash of guilt as his eyes took in the sea of flesh. He flipped through the pages as carefully as he had the *Catholic Digest*, but with much more attention this time. There were no articles about marriage in this magazine, and nobody who looked like they were about to whisk off to suburbia.

There were no women, either.

By eleven he wasn't feeling any guilt at all as he fumbled for the tube of lotion on his nightstand. By eleven-fifteen he had a pile of dirty tissues in his garbage basket, and by eleven-thirty he was asleep.

10

Hero

He dreamed of the bar. But this time he saw a window above the sign, and someone was standing there, watching him, surrounded by mist. He still couldn't see who it was, but he knew somehow that whoever he saw was beautiful and very sensual. Hal felt himself grow warm and then aroused, and with a soft cry, he reached out into the fog. He woke with a start, his hand outstretched toward the ceiling, his sheets sticky.

Shaking his head at himself but smiling, Hal tossed the sheets into the washer, downed some toast and coffee as he dressed, then grabbed his backpack, and headed out the door to catch his bus.

The site was already busy when he got there, more so than usual, and when he came around the corner and saw the series of dark, expensive cars parked along the curb, he winced. The days when the investors showed up to poke around were the worst. Well, he thought, at least today maybe they'd find out if Todd really was a spy. Thinking of Todd made him remember his hallucinated bar again, and he glanced toward the lot to see if the imaginary building was still there, but the lot held nothing but weeds and sand. Hal was trying to decide if he was relieved or disappointed when he felt someone tap him on the shoulder.

A tall, blond, and very chiseled man in a white suit was aiming a finger angrily at his face. "You," he spat at Hal. "You, boy, will come with me."

THE man had a thick accent that sounded vaguely European, and he looked foreign too: polished, chic, and slightly out of place, even for LA. The white suit didn't help. The only other person Hal had seen wear a white suit was Boss Hogg in *The Dukes of Hazzard*, though admittedly Hogg hadn't worn a delicate, exquisitely expensive, purple silk paisley button-down beneath his. There was also nothing

11

Roscoe P. Coltrane-esque about either of the thick and angry-looking men who flanked him. Their skin was as dark as their suits, though every now and again when the light shifted, Hal could have sworn their faces were red. *Really* red, like an angry tomato. And once he thought he saw horns.

Hal had his hard hat in his hands, and he flexed his grip against it as he frowned at the man in white. He glanced around as surreptitiously as he could, but there wasn't anyone else for this guy to be addressing. The man had turned around now and was striding across the site toward the trailer, leaving Hal little choice but to follow. The dark-clothed escorts sniggered at Hal before falling in behind him, and this time he knew he didn't imagine their faces turning briefly, brilliantly red. It didn't make sense, and it made him even more uneasy than he already was.

Gerry was waiting inside the trailer, but he was moving agitatedly around the narrow office, and when he saw Hal enter, his mouth flattened into a grim line.

"Hal." Gerry glanced at the man in white long enough to nod gruffly. "This is Mr. Eagan, the largest investor we have for this project." Gerry pulled his hand over his chin, grimaced, and then shook his head. "Hal, I'm going to have to let you go."

Hal blinked. "What?"

Gerry kept his eyes on his desk, and his voice was gruff. "Mr. Eagan says a guy he hired to keep an eye on the site caught you stealing."

Stealing? Stealing what? Hal looked at the man in white, but he was poking idly at his BlackBerry and not paying any attention. This didn't make any sense. Hal had just *gotten* here. He'd hardly been anywhere—his whole first day had been spent here in the trailer. He'd only been out yesterday, and he'd been stuck on that

12

damn wall for almost all of it until finally he'd volunteered to put everything away, just to walk around.

Which was when he'd imagined the bar. And seen Todd, who had acted strangely.

A guy he hired. Hal replayed his encounter last night with the shift manager before he left, and thought, *Fuck.* Todd *was* a spy. But this was horseshit! Hal hadn't taken anything—what was there to steal? Money? There was no money at the site! Why the hell would they keep money here? What else could he steal? Concrete mix? Rebar? He hadn't so much as lifted a pen, and he wouldn't. Ever.

Todd had acted strange when he'd heard that Hal saw something on the empty lot. What, did they think *he'd* taken the missing building?

"I don't understand," he said aloud.

Gerry looked at him at last with an expression that made it clear he didn't, either. He glanced again at the man in white, opened his mouth, and then shut it again, resigned. "I'm sorry, Hal."

Hal didn't know what to say. *I didn't steal anything* itched at the back of his mouth, along with *What the hell is going on, Gerry?* He and the foreman weren't close friends, but they'd worked together on a lot of sites, and he'd thought the man respected him at the very least. Why else would he have picked him for this project? *This doesn't make any sense* itched at his lips, too, but something in Gerry's expression made him pause. The foreman kept staring at his desk, head down, not looking at Hal and not at Eagan, either. Gerry, who liked to stand on top of the office trailer, surveying the site like God from the heavens. Gerry, who barked orders about this operation being "his ship" and how everything was "his call" and how anybody working on "his watch" wasn't taking any pussy tea breaks. But now Gerry was still and small and almost bent, and it was the man in white and his pair of goons who were looming.

Ah.

Hal turned to the stranger, still confused, still angry, but he felt himself fold up a little inside as he saw Eagan staring back at him. The man looked irritated, but in a bored way, as if he were willing to be patient for now but not much longer. *Languid*, Hal thought. The man in white was like his mother's cat that liked to lie across the back of the couch, tolerating Hal's presence until he was bored with the novelty of the invasion, and that was when he would lash out with his paw like a lightning strike and try to take out part of Hal's cheek. *I didn't do anything to you*, he had wished he could say to the cat, and he wished he could say it to the man in white now.

It was wrong. It was a mistake. It was really damn stupid. But Hal could see it wasn't something that talking or arguing or having a fit over would change. He looked down at the hat in his hands, staring at the dark stains in the creases of his fingers from the grease gun he'd worked with the day before, at the grime still caked on the edges of the brim of the hard hat. Then he set the hat down carefully on the desk that Gerry was still staring at.

"I won't keep you, then," he said, speaking slowly and deliberately to keep his pent-up emotion from leaking into his words. "Because I know you're pushing up against that deadline. But someday, if you get a chance"—His jaw tightened, and he couldn't keep neutral as he added—"I'd love to hear what it was I stole."

Gerry looked up at him then, his round face ruddy with indignation, and Hal felt reassured a little because he could tell it wasn't him the foreman was angry with. Then he cleared his throat and returned his focus to the desk. "Good luck, Hal."

And that was that. Hal took care not to look at the man in white as he turned around, and he headed toward the door, not sure what he was doing now but knowing he was damn well getting out of that office. But he hadn't taken four steps before Eagan spoke.

"I want him escorted off the property," he said.

"Look," Gerry said, in a tone that could have sliced concrete block. "I did what you wanted, and I fired him—but like he said, this is a busy day. I don't have time for this horseshit." The man in white raised an eyebrow at him, and Gerry glowered as he added an acid addendum. "*Sir.*"

Eagan gave Gerry a thin, bemused smile. "I wouldn't dream of troubling you, Mr. Harper. My men will see to his removal, but *you* will instruct your crew not to allow him anywhere near the site."

"I'll take care of it." Gerry sat down and started shuffling through paper.

Eagan turned to Hal, his smile dying away entirely. "As for you—I don't want to see you within so much as a mile of the site again. You will be escorted all the way to your vehicle, and we will inspect it for any further missing items before you leave."

Hal bristled, but he managed to push his anger back down. "I don't drive to work," he pointed out. "I take the bus." Which wouldn't be by for an hour, God help him.

This did not please Eagan, and for a moment he almost looked alarmed, but then his expression shifted back into a sneer. "It will be my *pleasure* to hire a taxi on your behalf, simply to see you off the site immediately."

"Keep your money," Hal said. "I'm taking the bus." He nodded to the goons and then resumed his march for the door.

"If you are found anywhere near the site," Eagan called after him, "*anywhere*, my men will take action against you."

You couldn't pay me to come back to this site, Hal thought, but he said nothing. He only kept heading for the door, down the stairs, toward the street and freedom.

But the goons followed even as he crossed the street and walked down the block, keeping just behind him. They stayed with him all the way to the bus stop, and when he sat down on the bench, they stood at either end of it like sentries, and it was clear they weren't going to move anytime soon.

Hal hunkered down on the bench and glared at the sidewalk. He wanted to pace, wanted to wander up and down the block, kicking and cursing under his breath while he tried to sort this out, to try and understand or at least to get rid of his anger, but he wasn't going to do that with these idiots here. So he just sat, stewing and hating. But after ten minutes, even that got old, so he sat back, opened his backpack, and pulled out a book. He wasn't sure how he was going to focus enough to read, but he might as well try.

However, when he saw the cover of the paperback he pulled out, he stopped. He had put a new murder mystery in there, he'd been sure of it: something he'd picked up last week at the grocery store but hadn't started to read yet. This book was not that book. It wasn't a book he had ever seen before, and it certainly wasn't something he'd ever buy. It didn't have a title, just a picture: a white fox standing in front of flowering tree. The cover was golden and embossed with all sorts of symbols he didn't know.

Hal glanced down at the backpack, worried that he'd picked up the wrong one somehow, but no, it was his—when he double-checked inside the flap, he saw the safety pin and the needle wound with thread he kept there, just in case he ever needed them. Hal shut the flap and then looked up at the pair of goons uneasily as he tried to hide the book with his arm. Was *this* what they thought he'd stolen? But the goons only gave him stony stares and went back to gazing straight ahead.

Hal looked down to frown at the book again, and what he saw startled him so much that he dropped the book. The strange fox book was gone, and his own paperback, *Cold Case in Cleveland*, tumbled over his knees and down into the gutter.

Shaking, Hal slid forward on the bench and reached down to pick it up. Something damn weird was going on, that was for sure. He grabbed the book, watching it carefully to see if it would change again, but it didn't. He settled back onto the bench with tentative relief and glanced up the street in the vain hope that the bus had decided to come forty-five minutes early today.

The bus wasn't there. But the bar was, standing innocently in the middle of the empty lot as if it had never left. And the woman in the fur coat was standing in front of it again. She saw Hal, smiled, and waved.

Then she crossed the street and came toward him.

CHAPTER 2
The Glass Palace

HAL dropped the book again and looked at his guardians to see what their reaction to the woman would be. They didn't even look at him this time, though. In fact, they were so still they looked like they weren't even moving. It was almost creepy, so Hal turned away, and by that time the woman had finished crossing the street, come down the sidewalk, and was now not even fifteen feet away.

She'd looked pretty enough from afar, but as she came closer, Hal found that she was nothing less than stunning. Beneath the fur coat she wore a pristine, white silk dress, and she had pearls in her ears. She had a strand of pearls at her throat as well, a string of white orbs, creamy and perfect, all the same size except a large one in the center of the choker. She was Asian, and her black hair was chin-length, smooth and sleek and shining. Her eyes sparkled, and her mouth was not pouty, not thin, but some magic harmony between, and when she smiled at him again, he saw her perfect, white teeth. Her face was narrow, and her eyes were close-set, her cheekbones high and her eyebrows thin. Her nose wrinkled a little, too, when she smiled. Which she was doing now.

"Hello," she said to Hal. "Lovely afternoon, isn't it?" She had a perfectly flat American accent, though even with that, Hal couldn't

18

shake the feeling that there was something extremely foreign about her.

Hal glanced at the goons again, but they were still just standing there, not moving. He looked at their chests and found himself letting out a relieved breath when he saw their chests rising and falling, albeit very shallowly and very slowly. He couldn't see their eyes behind their mirrored glasses, but he was somehow sure that they weren't looking at him or the woman. He was pretty sure they weren't seeing anything at all.

Hal turned back to the woman, who was looking at him patiently but expectantly. He gave up. "Can I help you?" he asked.

"As a matter of fact, you can." Her smile widened as she held out her hand, revealing manicured nails and a glittering diamond bracelet. "It's a pleasure to meet you, Howard Porter."

Hal accepted her hand uncertainly. So she knew his name. He looked back at the now-empty site again. "Look, if this is about the project, you really should talk to Gerry. They just fired me."

"This is a different project." She kept his hand captive, stroking it casually as she studied his face. Hal had to work not to yank back his hand. He looked again to his guardians, almost willing them to wake up now. But they remained frozen and silent.

"Howard Porter," the woman said, her voice full of silky wickedness, "would you like to hear your destiny?"

Hal glanced around. "Is this some sort of reality show or something?" God, that almost made sense, and as the idea bloomed in Hal's mind, he knew a moment of hope. He pulled back his hand and raised it with the other in front of his body defensively. "Look, lady, whatever this is, whatever your movie or TV show is about— I'm sure it's great, but I'm not interested, not today and not ever. I really just want to go home."

She laughed, and the sound was like a quiet cascade of bells. "I'm not from a TV show or a movie."

"Whatever it is, I'm still not interested." Hal turned away, first right, then left, and then he gave in and ducked between her and the goon at the right and headed for the sidewalk to find himself a bus stop away from the insanity.

And the vision hit him.

The Santa Monica street faded, vanishing almost entirely, and Hal saw instead a strange, surreal landscape of clouds and light. Not just light, but the purest, whitest light he had ever seen—brighter and sharper than the light of the sun, because it didn't come from the sun. It was simply there, in everything. And in the center of the clouds of light he saw a palace made of glass with a high tower in the center. The glass palace shone in the light, reflecting it like the diamonds on the woman's bracelet.

Someone was standing at a window in the tower. A man, a woman—he couldn't tell, and he didn't care. Whoever stood there was looking right at Hal, a hand held out toward him. Hal couldn't see the person's face or anything about them, but something about whomever it was tugged at him and made him yearn.

Hal's breath caught in his chest, and he reached out too.

But as if his movement had broken the spell, the vision faded, and Hal felt the loss like a blow. His hand was still extended before his body, reaching into empty air. The world seemed darker now, and not just because the vision of light had gone. The sky above had only one cloud, but it had moved over the sun, and Hal was cast once again into shadow. He blinked and then lowered his hand, but he kept staring at the place where the glass palace had been.

Hero

The bus stop was gone. The goons were gone. He was standing in the middle of foggy mist, and the woman in the fur coat was beside him, watching his face carefully.

"You had a vision," she said—a statement, not a question. "What did you see?"

The most beautiful person in the world, reaching for me from inside a palace of glass. Hal shut his eyes again, took a breath, and then shook his head. "Nothing. I didn't see anything." Stuffing his hands into the pockets of his jeans, he looked around, trying to decide which way to go, but all he could see was fog. Well, he'd just walk away then and hope he went out of it. He nodded gruffly at her. "Have a nice day." He walked off.

This time he managed about four steps before the vision came back. It was the same palace again, but this time something was wrong. The light was wrong, and the clouds were too big, too dark. Ominous.

Hal looked to the glass tower again, and he saw the shadowed person once more, reaching. The face was full of loss, hurt, and pain. Hal reached back once more, and once more the vision disappeared. But this time, when it went, Hal stepped forward, trying to follow—he stepped off the edge of the sidewalk and onto the street, twisting his ankle, and he went down in a great, crashing heap.

He didn't fight the fur-coated woman when she bent down to help him up, but he was breathing heavily now and looking around in apprehension. The palace was gone, and so was the mist. The pair of goons were still at the sides of the bench, frozen and silent, but this time, everything else was too. A bird hung eerily in midair above him. A car that had been barreling down the street toward him was stopped in its lane, the driver's mouth open in mid-sentence as he spoke into his cell phone. At the site, a backhoe's cascade of dirt had paused in its descent to earth about halfway down. Only the woman before him moved.

"Drugs," Hal rasped as sweat ran down the back of his neck. "Someone slipped me drugs."

"You are having visions," the woman said gently. "You are having visions of your destiny."

Hal was sitting on the curb, facing the empty lot where the bar had reappeared again. It was a strange, sagging building, and it didn't look right, like it was a flickering light that might blink out at any second. Hal rubbed at the back of his neck, at the sweat that was gathering there. "This is some sort of joke. Gerry or somebody is pulling a prank."

"There is no prank. Now, tell me, Howard Porter, what you saw in your vision," she said.

Hal stared ahead at the building, watching it swell and loom before him. "A glass palace," he said quietly. "I saw clouds and a palace made of glass, with a tower." He swallowed hard. "And a... somebody." He shuddered. "Someone very beautiful."

"Somebody who?" She dogged him, as if this were the important part.

"Just somebody." Hal shut his eyes and tried to remember. *So beautiful.* "I couldn't see who it was."

"Was it a man or a woman?"

Hal flushed, a deep heat that seared his skin, and he braced automatically. Oh, it had been a man. He would only have that kind of sensual longing for a man. But he'd just, out loud, said the person was beautiful. And he didn't like the edge to this woman's voice, the urgency in it. Why did she want to know? What business was it of hers? What was she going to do if he admitted it was a man he'd seen? Who would she tell? After everything that had happened to him today, was he really going to take that chance? Panic and shame made his flush deepen. He wasn't out, not to anyone, and he wasn't about to change that for this stranger.

He ducked his head. "I don't know." He swallowed, and then, because he knew he couldn't call her off any other way, he lied. "It was a woman." He blushed, again, this time from the falsehood, but he made himself look up at her. "A woman. Standing there like a princess in a tower."

That much was true. It was just that the princess actually was a prince.

She stared back at him, her dark eyes boring into him. She looked sort of stunned and then pained. She wiped her face clean and turned away. "The glass palace and tower are before you. And your... princess... is inside."

Hal raised an eyebrow at the bar. "It doesn't look like a palace."

"The trouble with visions," the woman said quietly, "is that while their general idea is almost always true, the actual details are, alas, a bit off the mark."

Hal stared at the building. This was weird, too weird to be real. It wasn't really happening. If he wasn't drugged, then he was asleep. This was just some dream. The woman wasn't real. The building wasn't real. The construction was too shitty, to start. The thing could come down at any second, by the look of the foundation. It was the sort of thing your subconscious put together. It wasn't real.

The woman bent down beside him. Hal could smell her perfume, something soft and sweet that made him think of movie stars. He tried to remember if he'd ever smelled in a dream before.

"I've been watching you, Howard Porter," she said. "You're a hard worker, and you're loyal. You treat other people with respect, even when they don't deserve it." She stepped a little closer, and he caught her scent a little more clearly: cinnamon and something woody. "You have a greater destiny than building condos. You want to build dreams. But you are so alone, Howard. So alone." She pointed to the bar. "The one who is inside that tower is alone too."

Hal shifted uncomfortably on the curb. His ankle was killing him, and he wished he would just wake up so this could be over. Because it was so obviously a dream. Even if that sort of thing were real—*him*? Nobody would ever go to him to rescue anybody.

But even as he thought this, Hal remembered the way the man had looked, and he shuddered. Guilt swamped him, and he wiped at his mouth to try to clear it. When that didn't work, he turned away.

The woman beside him leaned closer. "What's this?" Hal caught her peering at his throat, and before he knew what she was doing, she'd reached out and taken the charm on his necklace between her fingers. "St. Thomas." She looked up at Hal with sudden misgiving.

"Patron saint of construction workers," Hal said, pulling it back. "My mother gave it to me."

"And architects and cooks," the woman said, but she was still frowning. "The Apostle who doubted."

Hal backed away. "Look," he said, trying to be firm but not mean. "I gotta go home. Or wake up or sober up or whatever it takes to end this." But then he looked around and stumbled.

The bus stop was gone. The sidewalk was gone. The street was gone. He was standing in the mist again, but this time it was as thick as clouds, so thick he couldn't even see his feet. And the clouds were full of darkness.

24

Hal reached up and clutched at his medallion.

The woman took his shoulders gently in her hands and turned him toward the bar, which reappeared as she aimed him at it. It still looked the same: dingy and shambling and half-ruined. He looked up at one of the windows, thinking for a moment that he saw a face there, but when he blinked and tried to look more closely, he saw that it was only black, cracked, and broken, the glass taped clumsily in place.

"I'd like to wake up now," Hal whispered, his throat raw. "Please."

"You are not dreaming, Howard Porter," she said gently. "You are, in a way, awake for the first time." She urged him forward gently. "Come," she said. "You need to go inside and sit down. Have something to drink."

"Who are you?" Hal whispered as she led him toward the door. "What's happening?"

She inclined her head toward him. "You may call me Shinju," she said. "And I am here to guide you."

"Into hell?" Hal asked, looking again at the dilapidated building.

She looked amused. "To your destiny." She reached up and touched Hal's medallion again, and Hal felt it give and slide like water into her hand. Before he could protest, she held it out in front of him, and he watched, stupefied, as it melted into a golden pool in her hand and then reformed. She closed her hand before he could see what it was; then she lifted his hand and pressed the melted medal into his palm. Hal opened his hand, tentatively, and saw that his St. Thomas medal had been turned into a small golden coin with the image of a fox on the face.

"There are dangerous people inside, so take care. So long as they think you are a random stranger, they will only play games with you, but if they discover who you truly are, they will try to harm you. Tell them as little as possible, and above all, listen to your heart."

Hal stared blearily at the door, which was going in and out of focus. Sometimes it looked like a door, and sometimes it looked like a great black chasm with nothing more than a tiny silver strand bridging the gap between the sides. "I don't want to do this," he said. His words were slurring.

Shinju sighed. "I wish you had not been Thomas. I wish you were anyone but that one—well, I suppose you're better than Judas."

"*Hal*," Hal corrected. "My name is Hal." He felt very, very light-headed—almost drunk. *Over.* He wanted this dream to be *over.*

"No. Your name is Howard Abner Porter, whose patron saint is Thomas the Apostle. But whatever you are, you are all that I have," Shinju said sadly. "You are all *we* have."

The prince, Hal thought. He looked up at the door again, watching it flicker between plank of wood and gaping chasm.

"What am I supposed to do?" he asked. He turned to Shinju, but he decided there was something really wrong with his eyes or this dream was getting very, very weird because she didn't look human anymore. Her nose looked longer and darker, and she looked... furry.

"Go to Morgan," Shinju said, her voice soft and strange, echoing oddly in Hal's mind. She pulled his face down and pressed three kisses onto it, one on each eye, and one in the center of his forehead. "To Morgan," she whispered and let go.

Hal opened his eyes and saw that she was gone.

Hero

He looked up at the BAR sign, at the sagging building that sucked light, at the clouds that surrounded it. Then he looked at himself, plain and boring, covered with concrete dust, holding a golden coin in his hand.

It was a bad, bad idea, going into this building, whatever it was. It was a mistake, too, her choosing him—it had to be, because there was no way *he* was going to be able to help anyone. The strange accusations of the man in white paled next to the insanity of this, and for a moment, doubt consumed Hal, making the world even darker than it already was. He almost turned back to run wherever the clouds would take him. Then he touched the gold coin in his pocket, and he saw the prince in his mind again, smiling down at him from the tower, and Hal forgot that he wasn't good enough to save him, forgot that he'd told the fur-woman that he'd seen a woman instead of a man, forgot that this sort of adventure never happened to him, and the next thing he knew, he was opening the door to the bar and stepping inside.

HIS head was a little clearer as soon as he crossed the portal, and Hal took a steadying breath and stood in the entryway, assessing. The bar looked a lot better inside than it did from the outside, but it was still a sorry sort of place. The foundation had some pretty significant cracks, judging by the way the floor sloped to the large fissures in the walls, though someone had tried to cover those up with plaster. There were several brick pillars throughout the main room, which Hal could tell had been added after construction, and rather clumsily at that. They couldn't be doing much good. Instead of being placed to bear the load, they were just sort of scattered about, obviously pleasing someone else's aesthetic instead of actual architecture.

It wasn't even that great of an aesthetic, in Hal's opinion. The place was gloomy. The walls were painted a rich honey-brown that should have made the place look elegant but just made it dark. The lights were dim, and there were too few of them. There were too many tables crammed in, and the air was smoky, which was going to get the owner one hell of a fine if the police found out.

Of course, something told Hal that the police weren't even going to see a building here when they drove by.

Thinking this made him nervous again, and he tried to refocus on the structural defects because they were familiar and strangely calming. But the patrons inside the bar had started to notice him, and it was getting hard not to notice them back. They were staring at him and moving slowly closer—not unlike, Hal thought uneasily, dogs to the kill.

There weren't many people here, but they were weird. They were, technically, very beautiful, but they were also strange, even for California. Everyone was tall and lithe and lean, which was pretty standard, but there was something about their faces that put him off. They were *too* perfect, *too* sculpted. And they all had weirdly colored hair and strange clothes that looked like they belonged in some glamour version of *Lord of the Rings* with their tunics and glittering beads and skintight leggings.

Hal wondered, a little hopefully, if this was maybe some sort of movie set, but he didn't see any cameras.

Three people were approaching Hal, and he couldn't have said if they were men or women if he'd had a gun to his head and his life depended on his answer. All three were lithe, and all wore the loose, tunic-like garments; one had gleaming blue shoulder-length hair, one had short bright-yellow hair, and one could have doubled for David Bowie, but their faces were not definitively male or female.

He wasn't even sure they were human. He wasn't sure what that left, but "human" just didn't seem to fit.

Magical. They seemed magical. But whatever they were, he was pretty sure they didn't like him.

"Hello," the blue-haired one said, casting amused glances at his companions. "What have we here? A stray?"

The yellow-haired one giggled and put hand on hip, cocking the latter to one side. "It could use a bath."

Female—Hal would swear that one was a woman. He tried, surreptitiously, to check for breasts. Yes—a woman, definitely. The David Bowie one too. Maybe. Probably.

Hal cleared his throat and gave a curt, Midwestern-style nod. "Hello." He wasn't sure what else to say. He tried to remember what Shinju had told him to say and not to say. He couldn't remember a thing. Just that name. *Morgan.* He was supposed to go find Morgan.

"Uh—is Morgan here?"

The three exchanged glances, their penciled eyebrows lifting high into their brightly colored hairlines.

"Who wants to know?" the blue-haired one asked.

Hal checked the urge to reach up for his medal and clutched at the coin in his pocket instead. What was he supposed to say? The truth? If not the truth, what lie? What was he doing here, anyway? What was he trying to do? See Morgan—why? Who was Morgan? The princess? That made so little sense now, standing here. Clearly there was no princess, or prince, and if anybody did need rescuing here, *he* couldn't help them.

Oh Jesus. Hal took a quiet breath and then let it out. "A friend," he said, because he had to say something. "Morgan is… a friend."

This amused them a great deal, and Hal stood patiently, waiting until they finished laughing. The blue-haired one recovered first, waving his hands at his companions in a *wait, wait* motion.

"No, I think this could be fun," he said, breaking into laughter again at the end of his sentence. He wiped at his eyes, careful not to disrupt his eye makeup, and then nodded off to his right. "Take him over. I want to see what happens."

"Should we take him without Eagan present?" the yellow one asked, a little hesitantly.

The blue one sneered at her. "When Eagan is gone, I am in command of the Oasis. And I'm bored. I want to have some fun."

Eagan? These people were in league with the bastard from the building site? Hal managed to contain his expression, but his hands balled into fists. Eagan wasn't good news, but he wasn't here just now. *That* was good.

Except Hal still didn't know what the hell was going on.

The David Bowie woman came up beside Hal and linked her arm in his. "Come on," she said, her voice full of false sweetness. She made a face at his dirty clothes and then winked at the blue-haired man. "I'll take you to Morgan myself."

"I hope you're good with locks," the male one said, and they all three burst out laughing again.

Hal glanced over his shoulder at the door, wishing he dared just turn around and leave. He wondered if he even could.

Most of the room was watching them now as Hal's escort made a parade of their walk across the room; more strange, beautiful people with odd hair and painted faces laughed and pointed as Hal passed by or whispered behind their hands. The blue-haired one went before them, clapping his hands and calling out, "Attention,

attention!" to make sure their audience was as full as possible, and the yellow-haired one lingered behind, sniggering and occasionally goosing Hal to make the nearest tables laugh.

Hal, for his part, tried to remain nonresponsive, but while he managed to school his exterior, his interior wasn't so manageable. He wondered what kind of trouble, exactly, he was in. Was he going to die? He tightened his grip on the coin inside his pocket, taking comfort in its smooth heat against his sweaty fingers.

The David Bowie woman let go of him as they approached the bar, where a door led to what Hal would guess was a kitchen; he saw movement on the other side.

"Morgan!" Hal's escort called out, her voice sharp and mean, full of the singsong of playground teasing. "Morgan, someone's here to see you!"

Their audience laughed. Hal looked around to see who this Morgan might be, but all he saw was the bartender, bent over inside an open cooler, fetching drinks, leaning so far in that her skirt nearly tipped up over her bottom. Little silver chains dangled from the sides of the black leather garment, the only part of her visible beyond her legs. The blue-haired man leaned on the bar, bending sideways as if to speak to someone on the other side, though he kept his eyes on the eager crowd. "Yes—we think he might be your prince, come to set you free!"

Oh God, Hal thought, trying not to wince, feeling his face heat as the laughter swelled around him, and he braced, waiting for this Morgan to come through the door. But instead, the bartender climbed back out of the cooler and turned around.

And he saw the prince in the room of his tower, looking down at him in surprise, and a little confusion.

His face, his beautiful, perfect face….

Hal blinked and the vision faded, and he found himself staring, face to face, at the bartender instead. Except he *had* been wrong. This was the person from his vision—he could feel it in his bones—but this person wasn't a man at all. She was androgynous, yes, but she was decidedly female. She was looking at him warily, though she cast occasional, irritated glances at the crowd. She was very cute, in a comfortingly normal-looking way. She had dark brown, almost black hair, not weirdly colored at all. She wore a black leather vest and the black skirt full of chains, and she had silver bracelets on her wrists and another silver circle at her neck. She wore no makeup, though her lashes were very long and just a bit curled up at the ends. She was slender but slightly muscular, and she was normal sized, not impossibly tall like the other creatures in the room. The only thing odd about her was that her hair stuck out at crazy angles—it didn't look artful, just messy.

She wore *only* a vest. No shirt. No bra. And when she moved, he could see beneath it, and—yes. Absolutely, she was female.

And for the first time in Hal's life, the sight of a woman made him aroused.

The bartender glared at the blue-haired man. "Very funny, Talin," she said, her voice curt, but Hal thought he heard vulnerability underneath.

The blue-haired man pouted. "You're no fun anymore, Morgan. No fun at all."

"She's sore because Eagan's gone," someone shouted from the back of the room. "Or, rather, she *isn't* sore, not anymore, *because* Eagan is gone." Everyone laughed. Everyone but Morgan and Hal. But for Hal, it wasn't just because he didn't find the joke funny but because he was tugging at his ear; there was a strange ringing in it. It was a hum, and he realized now it had been coming and going for several minutes. It was driving him crazy. He looked around, but no one else seemed to notice it.

The blue-haired one raised an eyebrow. "Is it Eagan she misses?" He leaned over the bar, reaching out to stroke the bartender's cheek. "Or is it what he puts between her cheeks? Because that we can see to ourselves."

The humming started again, aggravated by the crowd's roar, but Hal's blood was already boiling at the mention of Eagan's name. This woman was that bastard's girlfriend? *Maybe not girlfriend. Maybe that's why she needs to be rescued.*

The woman who needed to be rescued slapped Talin's hand away. She turned to Hal, still glaring. "Well?" she demanded.

Hal swallowed, trying to put moisture back into his mouth. His ears, blessedly, were calming again. "Ah—can… can I have a drink? Please?"

"Oh, Morgan would *love* to give you a drink, honey," another heckler called out, and Hal tried to keep himself still and blank as everyone roared again and the bartender turned a deep, angry red.

But she was still glaring at Hal, and everyone else was laughing so hard, not paying him any attention, so Hal leaned forward just slightly and looked her in the eye as he mouthed, "I'm sorry."

He wasn't sure what he'd expected her to do, but he certainly hadn't expected her to look startled. But she recovered quickly, busying herself by reaching up above her head to pull down a glass. "What do you want?" she asked.

It took Hal a minute to register that she meant, "What do you want to drink." This was in part because the lapels of her vest gaped as she reached up, giving him a clear view of one very small, pert breast. And once again, he felt a rush of heat.

Well, he thought, as the vest fell back into place and the lust rolled away. *This is something different.*

"Beer," he said aloud, a little hoarsely. He glanced at the taps, but he couldn't see any labels or logos to let him know what this place served. "Please."

"Coming up," she said. She cast several glances at him as she drew his drink, still giving him that odd look.

The laughter had died down now, and Talin was leaning against the bar. He looked first at Hal, then at Morgan with a naked disdain and arrogance that both infuriated Hal and made him feel self-conscious.

"This ragamuffin, Morgan, says he is your friend," Talin said, once again loud enough for his audience to take in, and he paused to let the titters die down before he continued. "We thought we should bring him to you right away."

Morgan gave him a humorless smile. "How kind of you." She shoved the beer in front of Hal and then turned back to the cooler and whatever it was she had been doing before. But Hal saw her glance at him several times from beneath her arm, as if trying to make out who he was.

The David Bowie woman crossed her arms over her chest and pouted. "Morgan, you spoilsport! We want to see him try to free you. No one's tried in ages, and we're bored."

"Yeah, we want to see if he can break your chains!" someone shouted from the back.

Chains? Hal frowned and looked at Morgan again, specifically at her skirt and the silver chains that dangled there. But this time he saw her ankles, too, and her wrists. And that was when Hal realized the silver bracelet she wore was not a bracelet but a cuff, attached to a long chain leading to her other wrist, which was in turn attached to another chain, which then dangled toward the floor and her ankles to cuffs that circled her there as well. They were delicate, as thin as string, and they were joined in the center by a long silver chain that snaked across the floor, though what it was attached to back there, Hal couldn't quite see.

"Those are her marks of shame," the yellow-haired woman said, leaning in close to Hal's ear. "But then, you know that, don't you, since you came to save her?" She spoke in a mock whisper he was pretty sure they could hear on the other side of the room. The humming sound was back again, and Hal set his teeth against it. Maybe it was something with their voices?

"It's the prince, come to save the princess!" another heckler shouted, and they all laughed.

Hal couldn't help it. He reached up and pressed his fingers against his ear, shutting out the humming sound, which was now so loud it made him want to scream. It was when they spoke— sometimes some of the words cut into his teeth. "It's the prince," was fine. But "princess" echoed too loudly in his head. It *hurt*. His eyes were burning too. He blinked at Morgan, who had turned around again. She looked angry until she saw him, and then she came forward, worried.

Are you okay?

The others were laughing, but Hal heard the words inside his head. They made the buzzing quiet down, just a little, and he lowered his hand again. He cast a careful glance at Morgan, fairly sure it was her voice he'd heard, but honestly, he wasn't taking anything for granted anymore. She was watching him back, and as their gazes held, she lifted an eyebrow. Then he heard her voice again.

You can hear me? she asked.

Hal startled and blinked. His eyes darted to Talin, but he was too busy playing to the crowd.

You can *hear me*, Morgan said, sounding surprised. *That's... unusual. And you don't feel like a magician, though there's something magic about you.* She narrowed her eyes at him. *Your mind feels strange. You aren't* laumu, *and you can't be a Hunter.* She frowned. *What are you?*

How was he supposed to answer? Hal glanced nervously around, but the others were too busy enjoying their own jokes to pay him any attention.

Morgan's eyes widened, her expression leaning less toward confusion and more toward horror. *Oh no. You're human.*

Hal glanced around once more and then, very carefully, nodded.

Talin clamped a hand on Hal's shoulder as he addressed the crowd. "I think it should happen on stage, don't you?"

More laughter. Morgan was ignoring them all now, studying Hal with an intensity that made him want to squirm, but he held still, waiting to see what she would do. Because he was fairly certain she was about to do something, and every survival instinct he had told him not to get in her way.

He did, though, reach out and take a very deep drink of his beer. Then he took another.

She watched him drink. *They don't know you're human?* she asked, once more inside his head.

Hal paused and then very subtly shrugged.

She looked relieved, though only slightly. *Just don't try anything rash—just do what they say, and let me guide you, and you'll make it through okay. I still don't understand how you can mind-speak with me as a human, but we'll sort that out later. Tell me your name—just think it, very, very loudly. Don't close your eyes,* she added, when he did. *Just look into my eyes,* she instructed, meeting his gaze, *and imagine you can write the words on the inside of my head with your mind.*

Hal did as she asked, but he was a little distracted by how beautiful she was. He was thinking of her breasts, too, and her waist and her legs, which shocked and unnerved and aroused him all at the same time. *Maybe I'm not,* he thought, confused, but relieved too. *Maybe if it's the right woman, I'm not. Or maybe if it's just this woman.* He stared into her eyes, lost in them. Once again he saw the androgynous figure in the tower, only this time she looked like colors on an evening sky or stars in the heavens.

It's not the body I'm attracted to, he thought dizzily. *It's the soul.*

Her lips curled up in a wry but soft smile. *Your name,* she reminded him. And he knew, then, that she had "heard" every thought about her beauty and her body and her soul, and he blushed.

He forced himself to focus. Hal. His name was Hal. Except, as he let go, he felt himself going formal. *Howard. Howard Abner Porter. My name is Howard Abner Porter.*

Hello, Howard, she whispered back. The words felt like a caress inside his mind. *My name is Morgan, and I am the Oasis.*

Someone gripped his shoulder again. "Performance time!" Talin shouted, and abruptly the world went dark as a heavy, stinking cloth was wrapped around his head, and he couldn't hear Morgan's voice—or see her—anymore.

CHAPTER 3
Hal's Princess

HAL was dragged off the stool and herded through the room, blind and gagging on the stench of whatever it was they had thrown over his head. He briefly considered trying to break free or at least struggling, but there didn't seem to be any point, and Morgan had told him to follow her lead. But where she was, he didn't know. Was she safe? Was he still supposed to go like a lamb to whatever slaughter this was? Hal felt very ridiculous and angry and shamed. So he'd come in here to save her, had he? If anything, it looked like she was doing the saving.

He wondered for the thousandth time why Shinju had chosen him and what exactly she had wanted him to do. Maybe she hadn't. Maybe she was out there in the audience, laughing with the rest. It made more sense than anything else—this was some club, and they were having fun at his expense, and he was the idiot who believed their game. It *was* a reality show or a gag. Or something. It couldn't be *real.*

Except how the hell did Morgan talk inside my head?

They slammed him into a chair, cutting off his thoughts. Hal felt lights on his face and heat even before someone tugged the cloth bag from his head. Then the bag was gone, and for a moment, he couldn't see anything, just light. Then someone blocked it out—a shadow, the light making a halo behind them. Then Morgan was crouching down in front of him, looking sympathetic. Her chains were hanging from her, glinting in the light, one long one leading off the edge of the stage into the audience.

She also looked embarrassed.

I'm sorry, she said, inside his head again. She rested a tentative hand on his leg. *I'm not sure how you got in here, but it's clear you aren't a willing participant in their game.*

Hal nodded gruffly and then remembered he wasn't supposed to let the others know they were talking. He stared into her eyes, wanting to tell her about Shinju, about the vision, but all he could think was, *What is happening?*

She was very red-faced now. *It's a long story, and it's complicated. But essentially, they're making fun of me to amuse themselves. And now you are part of their fun.* Her hand tightened gently on his knee. *It was unwise of you to say you were my friend.*

Hal felt his groin twitch in response to her touch and, actually, to her look. It made him feel dirty and confused. *She's a girl, and I like her.* He felt like he should apologize, but he couldn't quite form the thought, and anyway, it probably wouldn't make sense. So he just sat there, waiting, watching, and… wanting. She was so beautiful. And the longer he stared, the more he forgot whether she was male or female, and he was simply full of desire for whoever this was before him. And when he unfocused his eyes and let the deep feeling take him, it surrounded him like a blanket, making the dirty, strange feelings go away. He felt clean and whole and good.

Then the audience hooted, and the beautiful moment crashed like glass to the floor.

There's only one way either of us are getting off this stage, Morgan whispered inside his mind, her hand sliding higher up his leg, drifting down toward his thigh. *And that way is to play their game.*

"Let the show begin!" someone shouted. "Warm him up, Morgan, so he can break your chains!"

Hal looked down at the silver line slithering across the floor, glinting in the glare of the stage lights. Were they even in the same room as they were before? He didn't remember seeing a stage near the bar. This thing was big and wide and open, and the building didn't look like it could support it. He forced his mind back on the chains. *They* didn't look like they'd withstand being stepped on. But something told him it wouldn't be that easy to break them.

They're magically bound, Morgan said inside his head again. *They are broken by words or powers of enchantment.*

"I'm no wizard," Hal whispered desperately.

She nodded. *I know. And they know too. You won't be able to break them, but their game is that you maybe do know, and I just need to try to coax it out of you. And they have specific ideas on how I should attempt to persuade you.* She glared off the front of the stage. *If Eagan were here, he wouldn't let any of this happen, and if a Hunter finds out there's a human here, things will get interesting very, very quickly. At least you're not a female.*

Eagan again. Hal frowned and glanced around. There were lights above them and a row at the edge between them and the audience, illuminating them both as Morgan came forward between his legs. Hal was confused but distracted by the way she was touching him and looking at him, because—well, he knew he had to be wrong, but it *looked* like—

Her hands slid up to his waistband, reaching for the button of his fly, and he hissed, pushing her hands away as he tried to stand.

The crowd roared and hooted, and Morgan shook her head, pushing him back down. She looked sad and embarrassed but also desperate.

"I told you," she whispered out loud, "they only let us off this stage one way."

Hal looked down at his waist, where her thumb was resting above the button to his fly. *One way.* She freed the button and then tugged down his zipper, and the crowd roared. Hal stared, his brain too stunned to react as he tried to process that this was actually happening to him. Beneath the dirty denim, however, his cock was hard and ready, already on board with this plan.

Then he looked at her sad face, and his erection vanished in a wave of guilt and anger. "In *front* of them?"

She nodded, looking so pained, so miserable—Hal was blushing hotly now, but it was more on her behalf than his own. They actually made her do this? How often? Dear God!

"I'm very sorry," she said, her voice quiet and small. *She* looked shamed now, and she couldn't meet his eyes. "They find it funny. I'm sorry." She smiled, a sad effort. "I'll make it as pleasurable as I can—I'm quite good, actually. And if it helps at all, if you close your eyes I can help you forget that they're here, and if you give me a picture, I can whisper to your mind that I'm someone else. I can even make you forget, if you like."

The buzzing was starting in his head again. Hal ignored it. "I don't need you to be someone else—I mean, you shouldn't have to do this! This is awful!" He waved his hand at the lights, at the crowd he knew was beyond them. "This is *inhu*—" He bit back the word and then swore under his breath and shook his head. "No. I won't do this to you. I don't care what their fucking game is—I *won't* do it."

"Do this—to *me*?" Now she looked confused. "You're worried about *me*?"

"Well, yes!" Hal was shouting now, and he gestured to the crowd. "God, I knew they were sick, but—" He swore under his breath. "I can't do this. I'd feel like a fat, clumsy bear with you in normal circumstances, and the—" *fact that you are a woman is still freaking me out.* "I never—I mean, I've *done this,* but never in front of people! It's—it's wrong!" He shook his head and backed away. "I can't do it."

She stood, blushing again, but she didn't look embarrassed this time. More overwhelmed and oddly hesitant. "It's okay—it's just a game. Usually it's with one of them, though, or Eagan. I'm just worried about you. Don't worry about me." She tried again to smile. "Just tell me who I should project for you. Imagine them, and I can replicate them. It's no trouble at all."

The buzzing was so loud now it made Hal nauseous. Something was hot in his pocket, too, burning his leg. He reached in and drew out the coin, but it was cold inside his hand. He clutched it as he shook his head at her.

"It *isn't* okay," he said, breathing hard against the pain. "I don't want you to project anyone for me, and yes, I am worried for you. This is slavery. This is—God, it's prostitution! You can't do this!"

The crowd was grumbling now. Morgan looked panicked. *Howard, please,* she whispered inside his head, her voice mingling with the maddening sound. *Please—just tell me who I can be, and I promise, you won't even know it's happening, and then I can get you out!*

"I don't want out!" Hal shouted. He clutched the coin in his hand so hard it cut into his skin. "I want *you* out! No projection! I don't want to forget—I want you out of here!" He stopped, suddenly dizzy, and he held his breath as the buzzing came to a crescendo and then snapped.

He heard a strange tinkling of metal followed by a collective gasp, and then a soft susurrus as the crowd began to whisper. Something released inside him, and he relaxed his hand, letting the coin fall from his grip with a heavy thud. When he opened his eyes, he saw Morgan standing in front of him, her face pale, her eyes wide.

Her chains, fallen from her body, were lying in a heap upon the floor.

THE room went very, very quiet. The only thing Hal could hear, in fact, was the sound of his own breathing. He still couldn't see anyone in the audience, but given what he'd observed of them so far, he didn't think they were going to be too pleased that their game had been cut short.

He could see Morgan fine. He was having a hard time looking at her, though—literally, he couldn't seem to keep his eyes fixed on her. Every time he tried he ended up looking at the floor or at the ceiling, or he'd close his eyes. It didn't make any sense. She was still there, and he could see her shape in his peripheral vision, but that was it. And it was making him crazy, because he didn't just want to see her face. He *needed* to see it. He tried once more— really, really tried—but found himself staring up at the black nothing of the ceiling again. He clenched his hands at his sides.

"I don't know what's going on," he said, trying to speak so only she would hear, though he doubted it was working.

"What did you do?" It was her talking, he knew that, but her voice sounded funny. He saw her move—he tried to look again, *forcing* his eyes to stay, and they hurt so badly that they closed on their own. He'd seen her, though, seen her face, and then he'd seen her frown at something glittering on the ground between them before bending to pick it up.

There was something wrong with her face. It wasn't her face. She looked, suddenly, very different. Like, *really* different. Like she was a different person.

Like she was—

His head started to pound, and he reached up, wincing. He gasped at the pain and then fell to his knees.

"What's wrong?" *Wrong.* Her voice was all wrong—it sounded nothing like it had been before! Nothing! He felt her hand on his shoulder. "Howard Porter, where did you get this? *How* did you get this?"

He forced his eyes to open and saw, blearily, the golden coin winking in her hand.

"Some woman did it," he whispered. "In a fur coat. It used to be my St. Thomas medal. She told me to find you." He shut his eyes and pressed his fingers to his head. "I had this vision of a palace. A glass palace. Then everything faded, until only this place was left. She gave me the coin, and I came inside."

"Oh no." Morgan let go of him, and he felt her move away. "*No.* She wouldn't."

Hal tried to lift his head, open his eyes, reach for her—anything—but the pain became so acute that he could only double forward, shrinking into the fetal position on the floor. His nose pressed into his knees, and he smelled and tasted wood. It was oddly grounding.

Heavy footsteps rocked the stage—Hal knew it was Talin before he even spoke. "What are you doing, slave?" His voice was tight, though Hal thought he was a little afraid too. "You have ruined the game. Put your chains back on."

"But that *is* the game," Morgan said. Hal had to shut his eyes and fight back nausea. God, there was something *wrong*—really, really wrong. And he thought Morgan knew it, too, because when she spoke, he could feel the tension in her voice. In that voice that wasn't hers but was.

"That is the game, to remove my chains," Morgan said again, gaining courage. "I didn't even have to coax him, did I? He but spoke, and my chains fell away. The game is ended."

She didn't sound like she bought that, and neither did Talin. Hal lifted his head and opened a bleary eye in time to see the blue-haired man smirk.

"Only Eagan may remove your chains," he said. "And he will be furious when he returns and finds what you have done."

"I've done nothing!" Morgan shouted, not hiding her nervousness anymore. "I played your stupid game—he's just some lost soul that wandered in here, and you know it. Let him go! I'll play with you when he's gone."

"No!" The word was out of Hal's mouth before he could stop it. He looked Talin in the eye, hating him so much his fingers curled against his palms. "Leave her alone!"

Talin stopped short, and Hal saw the shape that was Morgan pause too. The room, which had been buzzing with quiet excitement, fell silent once more.

"Her?" Talin repeated, quietly. He sounded confused.

Hal couldn't look at Morgan, but he could point at her. "Yes— *her!* Morgan! Leave her *alone!*"

His heart was pounding, but he stood his ground, ready to fight or be kicked or turned into a toad or whatever was going to happen now. He was ready for violence, though, which was why, when Talin burst into a cruel grin, he faltered.

"Her!" Talin, turned to Morgan, looked her up and down, then burst out laughing. "*Her!*"

"I think he's under a spell," Morgan said. *She* wasn't laughing. She sounded, in fact, very sad. And hurt.

Hal tried again to look at her, pushing past the headache, the nausea, and everything that doing so brought on. He could tell that something he had done or said had upset her, and this upset him. Why wasn't she happy that her chains had fallen away? He wasn't sure that he'd done anything to make that happen, but wasn't that good, regardless? He tried looking at her neck, because it wasn't her face and it wasn't her chest, but it proved as difficult as focusing anywhere else. He just couldn't do it—once again, after a few seconds, he found he was looking somewhere else again.

Talin stepped between them. Hal could look at him as much as he liked, unfortunately. Right now his irritating face was radiating smug amusement.

"Who are you, odd little man?" Talin asked—as always, projecting so the audience could hear as well.

"I'm Hal Porter," Hal said gruffly. "I'm just passing through."

"Yes," Talin said, a bit impatiently, "but from where to where? What breed are you? What clan?"

Oh shit. "I'm nobody special," Hal said.

"True," Talin agreed, "but even nobodies have clans and breeds. Are you fey? Do *not* tell me you are an ogre. We still don't have the stink out of here from the last one."

"Just let him go, Talin," Morgan said, pleading. Her voice sounded low; that was the problem. It had the wrong color. "Please—I'll play any game you want, but you have to let him go."

"I want to play games with your *friend*," Talin said to her, then turned back to Hal, smiling blackly. "I want to know *all about* your little friend who thinks you're a girl."

Hal winced as his headache bloomed in a sudden, angry burst and then reached up and pushed the base of his palm against his temple in a vain attempt to stop it. He heard Morgan shouting and pleading—*stop it! Stop, Talin, you're hurting him!*—but her voice only made the pain worse, and eventually, he fell forward again, clutching his head.

"Talin, stop—he's under a spell! You're going to kill him or drive him insane!" Morgan was weeping now, and every wrong note of her pleas and her sobs twisted the vines inside Hal's mind until he was clutching his stomach as well as his head, sure that vomiting was next.

Talin bent down beside him, putting his hard, beautiful face in front of Hal's as he made a closer inspection. "He's sweating—his pores are huge, and he's dripping with it. And that hair—so dull, so unimaginative. And there is *gray* inside of it." Hal saw, dizzily, the man's eyes widen as he made some sort of discovery, and he heard him swear in an unknown language as he rose.

"Human," he said, his voice full of hate. "He's *human*."

"Get a Hunter!" someone shouted, as the room filled with angry noise.

"No, please—*please!*" Morgan cried.

Hal said nothing, just rocked gently back and forth against the pain.

"No Hunters, not just yet," Talin said loudly, speaking over the din. "We will play a new game, one that will make everyone happy. Morgan, it seems, has some affection for this potential hero. And he did, in fact, somehow break the chains. *I* say we put it to the test. If he's human, he must, of course, be exterminated. If he *is* Morgan's savior, he must be obeyed. I say we solve the issue in one stroke. Or, as the case may be, with one drink. Let's give him the potion. Let's give Morgan's little human a Stiff Drink."

Hal only heard the beginning of Morgan's outcry—he registered her rage, and her terror, but mostly he felt his head split in two, and then he felt the contents of his stomach coming up through his body.

He must have blacked out because very abruptly he found he was sitting up again in a chair. Faces crowded around him, and the smell of something strange and acrid drifted into his nose. He blinked his eyes into focus and saw the David Bowie woman smirking as she held a smoking silver cup out toward him.

"Ah, the human is awake once more," Talin said from somewhere behind him. "And now we may begin the test."

"What test?" Hal looked around for Morgan—he saw her across from him, still impossible to look at. "What is this?"

"You broke Morgan's chains," Talin said cheerfully. "That means you are something special, more powerful than any magic that can come into the Oasis. According to legend, you have magic enough to transform the Oasis." His grin stretched wider. "Either that or you are just some strange, unlucky human, full of chaos, here to bumble your way into destroying our world. If you are magic, this drink Shira is holding will force you into your true form, and you will rescue your beloved from his cruel fate." He bent down so that Hal could see his wicked smile. "If you are human, you will blow up."

Hal began to sweat again. He glanced around at all the faces, all of which looked as darkly eager as Talin's. He still couldn't see Morgan.

"The sad truth," Talin said, not looking sad at all, "is that there is no hero. It's just a story Eagan told him to get him into bed and steal his power." He grinned. "However, you *will* blow up, if you're human."

Hal watched the air above the silver cup spark and sizzle, and then he shuddered and closed his eyes.

"Wait." He was starting to recognize Morgan's odd voice, but he kept his eyes closed so he didn't throw up again. "Wait—let me do it. Let me be the one to give it to him."

"No," the David Bowie woman said, sounding like a four year-old. "Talin said that I could."

"He'll blow up on you," Morgan warned. "All over your clothes and your hair."

The woman made a disgusted sound and drew back.

"Oh, let Morgan do it," Talin said, a little wearily. "On one condition: Service him, before he goes. At the very least—"

Hal didn't hear what else he said, because his headache came so fast and hard he passed out again.

When he came to, he was on the floor in a heap. Morgan was kneeling in front of him, holding the cup. Hal looked at it, not trusting he could look at her without passing out again, and that was why he saw the golden coin he had dropped slide very subtly from her hand into the bubbling liquid.

"Do you need help to sit up?" Morgan asked.

"No," Hal said, his voice dry and croaking. He pushed himself up carefully, keeping his eyes down. "Sorry—I can't look at you. It hurts. It hurts when you talk too. I don't understand—I'm really sorry."

"That's not your fault," she said gently. Sadly. She lifted the cup. "Drink it slowly," she said, pressing it to his lips. "It's very hot, and it will feel strange in your throat."

Hal wanted to draw back, but he knew they were being watched and that resistance would mean trouble for them both. He glanced around, but they had all apparently given him a clear path. *Because I'm going to blow up,* he remembered.

Just drink the potion, he heard her whisper inside his head. *I have a plan. I'm going to take care of you.*

Hal relaxed. Her voice wasn't wrong inside his head, and it made him feel better at once. He wished he could speak back to her, but he felt so chaotic, and to be honest, he was scared. Terrified.

"I'm sorry," he whispered.

He felt her hand touch his cheek gently. "I'm the one who should apologize." *And I will, soon. But first you must drink this, because they are watching. I know you have no reason to trust me, but I promise you, I won't let harm come to you.*

It was funny—Hal hadn't even considered that he shouldn't trust her until she brought it up, and even then he found he wasn't worried about her deceiving him at all. He didn't know why. All he knew was that he had this picture in his mind of somewhere soft and safe and private, and of Morgan there with him. He reached out and took the cup in his hands, placing them over hers, and drank.

It tasted fizzy, spicy, bitter, and slightly of orange. It reminded him of some soda he'd had as a kid, red and bright and strange, except there wasn't anything sweet about this. It was very hot, and it danced all the way down his throat into his stomach where it continued to burn. He felt the coin slide into his mouth with the last of the liquid, and then he stopped, spitting it back out into the bottom before handing the cup back to Morgan.

The crowd, on the other side of the lights, began to cheer.

Hal blinked and tried to look at Morgan again—he found, actually, that he *could* look at her now, but she was blurry at first. His stomach felt hot and strange, and the heat was permeating through his body, into his bloodstream, and from there to everywhere. His fingers were hot. His *brain* was hot.

His penis was hot and, in fact, was becoming quite erect. And that was when he realized he wasn't just hot. He was *aroused.* It was like his entire body was an erection. Hal glanced down at himself, alarmed and breathing fast.

Morgan stroked his arm in a gentling motion. "It's all right. I'll give you some ease in a moment. Just try to breathe through it."

Hal shut his eyes again and did as she said, but it was hard. "I feel weird," he said, panic rising. *I feel like I could pound nails. Into concrete.*

"The first stage is heightened arousal," she said. "We need to keep you in the first stage. The second is petrifaction. The third is explosion."

But the coin, I'm fairly certain, was part of the spell against you that changed how you viewed me. It should buy us some time, and it will help me get us out of here.

51

Hal saw the safe, warm place in his mind again, and he nodded.

"Take it out!" someone shouted from the back. "Suck it until it blows up!"

Hal opened his eyes again and looked at Morgan in silent question. He could almost see her now, and his headaches were gone. But something was still wrong, and it wasn't just her voice. She looked the same, but she looked different too. He couldn't put his finger on what it was, but something had changed.

Morgan smiled sadly and touched his face again. "Ignore them. They just think it's funny to watch us fuck, especially since you could blow up at any moment, as far as they know."

Hal was breathing hard now. He was still repulsed by the idea of doing anything sexual with Morgan for the benefit of these monsters, but the potion was making that more of an abstract objection than a specific one. He shifted against the hard bulge in his jeans—they were still undone from what she had started earlier, and he was pretty sure the tip of his penis was visible over the waistband of his underwear. He didn't even care. He was about, in fact, ready to reach down and start jerking himself off.

Morgan leaned in closer, her dark eyes fixed on Hal's face. "I'm going to have to play with you a bit," she said gently, apologetically, "until the spell builds up enough for me to use it. I'm sorry."

Hal shook his head. "It's okay—" He hissed and then gave up and grabbed himself. "I'm sorry. I don't like to be like this. Not in public. I would do it differently." He couldn't stop himself from adding, "Especially with you."

Morgan looked so sad. "Hal, I'm afraid you wouldn't do it at all with me if you could truly see. But there's no other way out now.

For that, *I* am sorry." She leaned forward and pressed a kiss against his jaw. "I can still project for you. And later, if this goes the way I hope it will, I can even change."

I don't want you to change, Hal wanted to argue, but then she was nibbling on his ear and sliding her hand beneath his waistband, and he could only gurgle and then pant. He closed his eyes again and fell forward against her, first nuzzling, then kissing her neck. She smelled so good—like fresh air and something spicy. Woman, man, whatever—he didn't care. For the first time in his life, it wasn't an issue at all.

She pulled his cock from his jeans, took it into her hand, and Hal moaned into her ear. Then he heard the catcalls from the audience, and he tried to draw back.

Morgan held him in place. *Just a bit longer,* she whispered in his mind as she trailed her mouth back up his jaw, toward his mouth, nibbling on his chin. Hal groaned and opened his mouth over hers. He heard the hoots and jeers and calls for them to *fuck faster!* in the distance, but he ignored them, which the potion was making it easier to do with every passing second. God help him, but he *would* fuck her right here, right now, he was so goddamned horny. And she tasted so good. He suckled on her tongue, loving the way she shivered, and he did it again as he ran his hands down her sides. He slid his hands over her breasts, trying to take them in his hands. For some reason this didn't quite work, and it confused him. Then the heat surged in his blood, and he didn't think anymore, just grabbed her nipples and squeezed them hard.

She gasped and then rocked against him. The crowd roared.

Hal pushed deeper into her mouth and lifted a hand to run it up the inside of her thigh.

She stiffened. *Wait!* he heard her cry inside his head, but he didn't wait, didn't stop, because he couldn't. He slid his hand under her skirt and—

—froze.

The heat was still pounding inside him, trying to override, but his brain was shutting down everything now, trying to process this, trying to write the program over until it made sense, but there was no making sense of this. Hal let out an unsteady breath, shifted his hand, and then froze again.

It was still there.

Morgan drew back, wincing and blushing. "I'm so sorry. I'm so sorry."

The crowd was laughing, and clapping, and hooting—horrible, horrible laughter that was all *at,* none *with,* and it cut almost as hard as the contradiction of what Hal's brain knew and what his hand knew too. He blinked and pulled back, looking at her again. *Really* looking. At *her.*

But with every passing second, he knew he was wrong, that he had been wrong all along. He could see all of her now, not blurry, not masked, not even veiled by his previous conviction. He saw what he could not see before, for whatever reason. The subtle angles. The definition of the shoulders. The flat chest. The Adam's apple. And it all went together like pieces of a puzzle, cinched into place by what Hal had, unquestionably, felt beneath Morgan's skirt.

Morgan was not a woman. Morgan was a man. Hal was saving a prince after all. He had been attracted to a woman, yes, but not really, because this woman was a man. He was making love, in public, to a man.

Out? Oh yeah. He was out. To a room full of cruel strangers, who wanted to see him blow up.

And to Morgan. *Who he'd just called a girl, in front of everyone.*

Hal stared at her—his—face, got lost in the confusion, and forgot to breathe.

Morgan blinked, a long, slow gesture full of shame. "I'm sorry," he whispered. "I didn't realize what she'd done until too late. I'm so sorry."

She—that could only be Shinju. Hal shook his head. "How could she turn you into a woman?" he demanded. *And why the hell would she do that?*

"She didn't," Morgan replied. "She cast an illusion. It was linked to the coin." So sad—she sounded so, so sad.

He. Hal clenched his hand at his side—the hand that had gone beneath her skirt. *His* skirt. Jesus. This was so fucked. Except now it made sense. He'd gotten hard for breasts, yes—illusions of breasts on a man. He laughed at himself, bitterly.

"Come on—fuck him!" someone shouted.

The shout jarred Hal, and he couldn't help it—he drew back. And he regretted it instantly, because Morgan's face, already pained, tumbled into misery like he'd never seen before. Then it went completely blank.

"Don't worry," Morgan said kindly. "I won't. You've been upset enough. I think I have enough reserves built up now, anyway."

Hal wanted to argue, to point out she—he—had been upset, too, to confess that, actually, he should explain a few things about himself. But his arousal was starting to turn to pain, and he could only huff and hiss.

Morgan reached forward and gently took Hal's hands. "I have to pretend to kiss you," he said quietly and leaned forward. "Then it will be over."

You can actually kiss me, Hal thought, and there was no shame, just yearning. But he didn't think Morgan could hear him, and before he could try to repeat it, he was leaning forward. Hal shut his eyes, not caring, just waiting for the touch of his lips and the release.

It never came. As Morgan bent closer, Howard felt the coin slip between his fingers again, and then, with no warning at all, the world blew apart and he was gone.

CHAPTER 4
Morgan's Room

HAL, however, did *not* blow up.

This surprised him more than a little. If there had been time, he would have braced or maybe even said a final prayer. Or something. But he hadn't died, and he was no longer half-naked on stage in front of a tribe of assholes. He didn't know where he was, but he knew he was lying on a soft surface, that it was quiet and warm, and that it felt safe.

And Morgan was here. Hal couldn't see him, but he could hear him. There was a curtain on the other side of the small room, an orange-pink silky thing hanging on a thick piece of string, and a shape was moving behind it, fussing with something. Hal knew it was Morgan because he could see his silhouette: the spiky hair, the leather vest gaping open, the skirt. He waited to maybe hear him speak inside his head again, but then he supposed there was no need in this place; it was just the two of them.

Hal looked around the rest of the room. It was a small bedroom, reminding him of a college dorm, containing not just a bed but a whole life. The walls were cracked, worse here than they had been in the bar, and the ceiling was peeling, but the damage had been draped by swaths of richly patterned if faded tapestry and accented by beads. There was a vaguely Japanese feel to the decor, but mostly it was just random and old. Heavy wooden shelves were pressed up against the fabric walls, reaching all the way to the ceiling, and they bore all manner of exotic trinkets of varying worth. There were gold bowls and china boxes, but there were also wicker baskets and wooden utensils. Hal saw tools as well, ancient but highly utilitarian, and they were stored neatly on faded gold velvet, making them look even more like pieces from a museum.

There were no windows, and as far as Hal could tell, no doors. He tried imagining there was one behind the curtain, but when Morgan came around, it shifted, and he saw that this wall was solid too. He looked up at the ceiling, but aside from the cracks, it was smooth, and unless there was something under the floor—the floor covered with a huge, threadbare carpet anchored by seven heavy shelves, a dresser, and the bed Hal was lying on—there was, in fact, no way out.

"Sorry, no, there isn't a door," Morgan said, following Hal's increasingly frantic search for an exit. He leaned against a bookcase near the bed and ran a hand self-consciously through his hair. "I've never realized it would worry anyone, because I've never brought anyone here before, except my mother."

Hal did his best to shelve his panic, but the trouble was there were only two things to focus on: the exit-less room or the man-who-was-not-a-woman who had brought him here. He gave up and stared at the ceiling. "Where are we? What—what happened?"

"We're in my—well, room, I guess you'd call it." Morgan ran his hand through his hair again. "There is one place in the Oasis no one can access but me, and this is it. I haven't been here in a while, so please excuse the mess." He reached for something on the bed and stuck it quietly onto a shelf, his eyes still roaming the room, scanning for other things. Occasionally he moved other things out of sight as well.

Hal watched him, braver now that Morgan wasn't watching back. He could still see the woman in him, vaguely, but there was no mistaking now that he was looking at a man. A young, handsome, effeminate man, but he was a man, regardless. Hal could see the definition in his arms, his face, his legs, even through what sure as hell looked like a pair of tights to him. It was so obvious now that he felt embarrassed. And confused. Hal felt really, really confused.

And shamed. The old demon was back, pressing on him harder than ever.

Hal had known for ten years that he was gay—probably longer, if he were honest—but it was when he was twenty-two and he came home too early to the bachelorette party his sister was hosting that he truly admitted it to himself. She'd hired a stripper, and the man was wearing nothing more than a thong as he humped the drunk and giggling bride-to-be on a chair in the middle of the room, and Hal had walked into the scene. They'd laughed for days about how shocked he'd looked, how pale he'd gone, but they thought it was just shy Hal being prudish.

He hadn't been feeling prudish, though. He had felt *aroused,* really, really aroused, like he'd never felt before. He'd lain in bed that night, clutching the rosary he hadn't so much as touched since he was confirmed, saying Hail Marys and praying to God to take this feeling away. He'd tried so hard to talk himself out of what he'd worried he'd known about himself for years. He'd tried dating, had even tried a hooker once, which had been even worse than dating— but it was that night and that dancer when he'd finally given up. He was gay. There was no way around it. And none of his prayers had ever been answered. He was going to stay gay, and that was that.

He didn't feel it was a sin, really. He knew he should think of it that way, according to the church, but he couldn't change it no matter what he did, so how could it be his fault? But he didn't like the way other people would talk about him if he came out. He didn't like the way people would whisper, and he knew they would. It was the other reason he'd come to Los Angeles. Surely here, in a place this far removed from Kansas, he thought, he could be comfortable enough to be himself.

But it hadn't worked out that way. By the time Hal hit the gay bar scene, he was too old, and to be honest, he'd have been almost too shy even when he *had* been young enough. And really, it had been just like construction. You'd think it would all be different here, but it was just bigger and stranger. So he'd turned into something of a monk, dating no one, approaching no one, thinking about no one, except for when it all became a little too much, and then he jacked off in bed and wished he were the sort who could hire a rent boy. He'd resigned himself to his fate and tried not to think about it.

Now, though.... Hal looked up at Morgan, who was still fussing on his shelves, more out of nervousness, Hal suspected, than because he wanted to clean up. Now, somehow, Hal was here, with this strange, beautiful, *magical* man. In a room with no doors and no windows. He was with a man who could cast spells and read his mind.

He was with a man, he thought, as Morgan's eyes came back to him, who had already fondled him, and kissed him. And seemed to like it. And Hal had liked it too.

Their eyes met, and Hal quickly looked away.

"I'm sorry," Morgan said very quietly. "I truly am."

Now Hal *had* to look at him. "Why? You didn't do anything. I'm the one who was an idiot."

"It wasn't your fault she enchanted you," Morgan said with a little heat. Looking miserable, he sank a little lower against the bookshelf. "I'm so sorry, for all of this."

Hal jerked his head at the foot of the bed as he shifted to make room. "Sit. This place looks unstable as hell, and you're going to knock that case of gewgaws over."

Morgan stood, rubbing his arms as he glanced around at his room. "Does the Oasis look that bad?"

Hal grimaced at the cracks on the wall, but he was feeling a little easier. Construction, now, he could talk about all day. "Aside from having no door, it just doesn't look well-designed. I don't understand what's bearing the load. And don't even get me started on that bar downstairs, and that stage. Who built this place, anyway?"

Morgan blushed, rubbing his arms again. "I did."

"You mean you designed it?" Shit, he'd just insulted an architect. Well, it wouldn't be the first time.

"No—I made it. Eagan designed it, I built it, and I am currently failing to maintain it. Part of the problem is that he's always *changing* everything. It makes it so hard to keep things in proper order." He gave Hal a curious look. "Shinju didn't tell you *anything* about me? She said, 'go get the woman,' and off you went?"

Hal grimaced and shifted uncomfortably on the bed. "It wasn't exactly like that," he grumbled, but quietly, because it was sadly close to the mark. "I don't really understand it, to be honest. It started yesterday when I was getting off work, and there was this woman in a fur coat standing outside this bar that hadn't been there when I'd passed by the lot in the morning."

Morgan winced. "She *exposed* me? How many people saw?"

"Just me, as far as I could tell," Hal said. "But I didn't see you. Just the building."

"That's not possible," Morgan replied. "There's no way only one human could see, if she lifted the enchantment on the Oasis."

"What is this Oasis everybody keeps talking about?" Hal asked. "Is that the name of this bar?"

Morgan gave him a strange smile. "The Oasis is me. That's what I am, Howard."

Hal frowned. "You're a bar?"

"I am this place. You are a human, and I am a place. And before you say that I look human, that is a guise. I'm a shape-shifter, like everyone else in the bar, but I'm different, because I am the place they live in. Think of it as if the house you lived in had a heart, or a soul, and it could walk around and sit at the table with you." He gestured to the room around them. "This room is my inner sanctum. It has no doors because only I can come here, and I don't need doors to enter it. It's been harder to come here lately, because I'm getting weaker, and it took considerable effort to bring you here as well. It's harder for me to change my appearance too; I can only modify what I suppose you'd call my 'human form.' But the spell Shinju cast—well, you could say I hijacked it. I used it to cancel out the effects of the elixir, then the rest to bring us here. Talin and his idiots can't reach you. We're safe."

Hal wasn't exactly sure he understood—he was trying to imagine someone giving birth to a bar, and it just didn't work—but he nodded anyway, because he understood enough to get that whatever was going on was magical, which was jarring enough. That he was standing here talking to a very attractive house was more than he could process.

"Why were they so upset when they found out I was human?" Hal asked.

"Because humans are dangerous," Morgan replied. "Humans aren't ruled by magic. They can be manipulated with it, but even that is a dangerous business. For magical creatures, you're like wild cards. We never know what you're going to do to us."

Hal lifted an eyebrow at him. "*You* don't look too worried."

Morgan's grin was briefly wicked. "I wouldn't mind anything you did to me, Howard." When Hal blushed, Morgan looked away, his smile fading. "I guess it's encouraging that she's still trying to get me out." He was staring at the floor now, not looking very encouraged. "Though I still can't believe she made you think I was a woman."

That was clearly bothering both of them. Hal wished he knew what to say. He wished he knew how to explain that, actually, he liked him so much more as a man.

"Look," Hal began, carefully. His voice shook a little as he went on "About that. I don't"—his face heated—"I don't really care that you're not a woman."

Morgan glared at him. "I saw your face," he snapped. "You were *appalled*."

"I wasn't appalled. I was *surprised*." Hal ran a hand over his hair and then nodded at Morgan. "What's up with the skirt, anyway?"

"It's not a skirt." Morgan glanced down at himself, brushing his hands across the ruffled leather. "Well, I suppose it's skirtlike. I just don't like to wear *laumu* clothing, is all. And when they want.... Well, it's just easier if it doesn't take a lot of shifting drawers to let them—" He cut himself off and tugged at his hem. "It really looks like a skirt?"

It did, but Hal was suddenly loath to agree. "It looks good," he said instead.

Morgan sank down on the foot of the bed, looking miserable again. "I'm sorry I helped convince you I was a girl, however accidentally." He brushed his hand over his leg and leaned against the post of the bed. "*Really* sorry."

Hal felt guilty again. He wanted to explain, but he didn't know how, not without knotting himself up. He watched Morgan instead, taking in his profile, the slope of his neck, the gentle curve of his shoulders, and he found himself, once again, becoming aroused. He cleared his throat. "Tell me what's going on," he said, to change the subject. "Who is Shinju? Why did she send me here? And why does that upset you so much?"

"Shinju is… complicated." Morgan smiled sadly and drew his feet up onto the bed, tucking them back behind him as he shifted to face Hal. "And it upsets me that she sent you here because she shouldn't try to bring me back, and yet I know she's always going to. Because I'm trapped here because of my own stupid mistake. I used to blame her, and I wish I still could. But it's my own doing. And it means there's no way out."

"What was that game they were playing?" Hal asked. He shifted on the bed, feeling twitchy. "You told me they were waiting for your hero to save you, to break your chains."

"It's a cruel joke. There is no hero," Morgan said. "No one can set me free."

"I broke the chains," Hal pointed out.

"Yes—you did so using part of Shinju's spell." Morgan grimaced. "There *is no hero*, Howard. There is no one who can drink the elixir of light and live—*I* can drink it, and they do love to give it to me, because it makes me… more interesting. That's all it's

64

ever been, just Eagan's concoction to enhance my status as a whore. But to anyone else it's poison."

"I met him," Hal said, stiffly. "Eagan. He got me fired from my job this morning."

Morgan looked wary. "And he let you come here?"

"I don't think he knows I'm here. He had his thugs escort me off the building site. I was waiting for the bus when Shinju appeared, and then... well, I don't really know what happened, but I ended up here."

"But he saw you as a threat." Morgan looked confused. "And you aren't a wizard, honestly?"

"No. I'm a construction worker."

This didn't seem to mean anything to Morgan, and for a moment they regarded each other in awkward silence.

After awhile, Hal cleared his throat. "That's what that thing was called? The elixir of light? That sounds... pretty."

"It's another one of Eagan's cruel little jokes," Morgan said. "Most of them call it a Stiff Drink, because of what it does." He frowned absently. "Usually I do too. I don't know why I called it that, 'elixir of light.' I suppose it's all this hero talk." The frown became a grimace. "That's how he trapped me, you see. He told me the elixir was a magic potion that would free me and turn me into whatever I wanted to be. He told me it was the sun trapped in a bottle. He said that if I drank from it, I would never be lonely again." He sneered down at the bedspread. "He lied, and he didn't. I'm 'free,' but he didn't tell me that I would be whatever *he* wanted me to be, or whoever gave me the drink. Mostly they use it for sex, but they are siphoning most of their magic off of me anymore, and it's all because of the bargain I struck with Eagan, and the power of that drink. I would never be lonely, either, because I would be a slave for the rest of my life. But that's Eagan for you. He loves to play games with your head. He loves you to think you're about to get away, only to surprise you at the last second with another length of chain. He enjoys watching hope turn to despair. He thinks it's very funny."

Hal remembered the way Eagan had lounged in the foreman's trailer, bored and recumbent while Gerry had been stiff and squirming and he, Hal, had been confused and hurt. *And even that, he realized with some horror, was just enough to be mildly amusing.*

Hal rubbed at his arms, suddenly feeling cold. "How did I live, if that potion was supposed to have killed me?"

"I extracted it, using your charm. It's complicated to explain."

"My St. Thomas medal that Shinju enchanted?" Hal asked.

Morgan raised his eyebrows. "Oh no. She didn't enchant *that*. That coin carried *your* magic, Hal. The magic you gave it."

"My magic?" Hal repeated, dubious.

"The belief you carried for it," Morgan said. "It was very strong. So strong that it allowed me to bring us back here."

"But not enough to free you," Hal clarified.

Morgan nodded sadly and then drew his knees to his chest. "I used to believe in the hero," Morgan said quietly. "I knew even when Eagan told me there could be someone who set me free that he was lying, but I used to dream of him anyway. A prince to come and save me. To love me. He used to be what kept me going, what I lived for. But not anymore."

He looked so sad, so lost—it broke Hal's heart. But Hal also saw, as his eyes drifted to the gap between Morgan's legs, that those tights didn't go all the way up, gathering instead with elastic at the tops of his thighs, and they were held up with garters. He saw that Morgan actually wasn't wearing anything under his skirt. And he remembered what he'd felt on stage, beneath that leather. And he began to feel warmer and more snug inside his jeans.

Before he knew what he was doing, he was reaching out, touching Morgan's foot tentatively. When Morgan only pushed his foot a little closer, Hal slid his hand to his ankle and squeezed.

"Let me help you," Hal said. He ran his thumb over skin and bone, stroking, not embarrassed or self-conscious at all, which surprised him, but even this was some distant sort of reaction. It felt good to touch Morgan. He didn't feel guilty because Morgan was a man or awkward because he had thought Morgan was a woman. In fact, he didn't feel anything right then but a low-grade, pleasant arousal. "Tell me how I can help you."

Morgan shook his head. "There's nothing. I'm not trying to be rude, but as a human—"

Hal's hand slid up to his calf, and Morgan paused. Hal did, too, and looked down at his hand, wondering, a little absently, what he was doing. He drew back, self-conscious. Then he felt something fizzle inside his brain, as if there were some sort of capsule inside that popped open and gave him a new chemical command, and he put his hand back again.

Lust. He felt lusty and—horny. He felt very, very horny and itchy. His fingers brushed against the silk of Morgan's tights, the warmth from his skin beneath making him even more aroused. *So he's a guy,* Hal admitted to himself, giving in to the feelings swelling inside him. *You've only looked at guys for years. Isn't it time you touched one again?* He shut his eyes and drew a long, slow breath. The guilt, the fear, the shame—it was all gone. Somehow, right then, it didn't matter. Maybe it was a spell. Maybe it wasn't. Maybe that potion was still inside him. Maybe he was going to die, after all.

But what a way to go.

Hal opened his eyes. He felt no guilt, no shame. *Nothing.* God, it was so wonderful! He almost cried it felt so good, but he was too busy feeling horny as hell. Oh, he wanted Morgan. He wanted him like he'd never wanted anyone or anything. He didn't care what this potion might do to him. He'd take a whole pitcher full of it to keep feeling like this.

Feeling as if he were in a dream, he slid his hand up the side of Morgan's leg, up over his knee, and onto his thigh, to his bare skin.

"Howard?" Morgan said, a little hoarsely.

"Mmm?" Hal said, watching his hand's ascent. He caught sight of the edge of Morgan's skirt, and he smiled.

Morgan let out a shuddering breath. "What are you doing?"

Hal stopped, his fingers just nudged beneath the hem. He looked up at Morgan and found himself pleased by the softness and desire he saw in his eyes.

Morgan winced. "Oh no. I didn't get all of it—you still have the potion inside you!"

Hal grinned. "Yeah, that's what I was thinking." His hand slid higher.

Morgan pushed him back, but weakly. "But I was so sure! I *know* that I used it all—that was the only way to get us here! It shouldn't make you like this! It should be—*ah!*" He shut his eyes and leaned forward as Hal's hand evaded his and slid beneath the skirt, sliding up toward his pelvis. "Howard," he whispered, nervous, even as he shifted his leg to give Hal better access. "Howard, please—you'll be upset about this later. Assuming you live that long."

"I don't think I'll be upset, no." Hal slid his hand around the back of Morgan's hip and tugged at him. Oh God, it felt so good to be free. He grinned. "Come here, you."

Morgan slid forward on the bed until he was practically on Hal's lap. His eyes were heavy with passion, but he looked sad too. "You will be sorry. You don't want this. You were attracted to a woman, before. This is just the potion. I can see it in you now—it went deep inside you, somehow."

Oh, no, it's not the spell. I've wanted this my whole life. "Am I going to die?" Hal asked, unconcerned.

"Maybe." Morgan flushed and then set his jaw. "No. I won't let it kill you." Morgan closed his eyes as Hal slid his hand up toward his neck, curling his fingers around his spine. "But I can't draw it out of you the same way before. We'll have to…." He bit his lip and then leaned into Hal's massaging hand. "…be more direct."

"And how's that?" Hal said, still not upset because he was too busy examining the flaps of Morgan's vest, considering if he wanted to push them aside or just apply his mouth directly to the center of Morgan's chest.

"Sex," Morgan said, very softly. "I'll draw it out of you, but it will be during sex."

"Okay," Hal said and tugged Morgan's hip to haul him up onto his lap.

He sat Morgan directly on his erection, which was still captive beneath his jeans, and Morgan trembled and then sagged against him, pressing their foreheads together.

"You will hate me," he whispered.

"I won't ever hate you," Hal said, and he knew somehow that this was true, that this part of him wasn't enchanted in any way. It unsettled him a moment, and then he caught a whiff of Morgan's scent, and lust carried his uncertainties away again.

"It will be different sex," Morgan said, but he was stroking Hal's cheeks, and breathing hard. "Not what you're used to."

The only sex I know is full of uncertainty and shame. "Sounds good," Hal said, and cupped Morgan's buttock in his hand.

Morgan gripped his shoulders and pressed a kiss against his ear. "This isn't you," he whispered. "This isn't real."

Yes it is, Hal thought, but nuzzled him back instead. He wanted to tell him, to explain, but he couldn't find the words.

"You're so gentle. And so kind." Morgan laughed, the sound quiet and sad. "You're going to break my heart."

No. I'm going to save you, Hal thought, drunk on the drug coursing through his system. *I'm going to find a way to save you. I don't give a damn if you're a man or a woman or a house or a mountain. I'm going to save you.* But he knew he couldn't say this, that Morgan wouldn't believe him.

So instead, he turned his head, found Morgan's mouth, and kissed him.

SPICY.

Morgan tasted spicy and soft, like rainwater. Hal slid his hand over Morgan's stomach, loving how it trembled as he touched Morgan's skin. He slid his palm up to close over Morgan's nipple. Morgan shivered and then laughed, but it was a sad sound. Hal lifted his head to ask him what was wrong, but Morgan only traced his finger against Hal's cheek and then kissed him again.

This time the kiss was deep and carnal, and Hal wasn't shy about running his hands all over Morgan, who soon stopped acting anxious and began feeling him back. Within minutes they were both breathing hard and tugging at each other's clothes.

"I want this," Morgan confessed in a whisper as he fought against Hal's buttons. His lips brushed against Hal's as he spoke. "I want this so much."

Hal felt very much the same way. His erection was like a brick in his jeans, heavier and harder than it had ever been. He felt like he'd felt in the bar, but not as scared or wild—just hot and hard. This—being with Morgan—felt better than anything had ever felt. The feeling of rightness that seemed to go hand in hand with Morgan was increasing a thousandfold with every passing second. And he wanted him. He wanted him *now*. Hal began to fumble at Morgan's skirt, shoving it up. He began to feel urgent, fixated on getting Morgan's cock exposed, and his own. It was as if now that he was freed he was in a frenzy, and he could not make love to this man fast enough.

But just as he was reaching for his belt, a sharp surge of pain came out of nowhere. Hal gasped and then grunted as his vision went red, and he clawed at Morgan's thighs with his nails. His breath was coming fast—too fast—and he couldn't focus, couldn't control. There was another surge, and he saw red and then *felt* red. He grunted again, and began to claw at the zipper to his fly. He had to get it *out*, or he swore he was going to explode.

"It's coming on too strong," Morgan said, coming out of his own sexual coma. He pressed his hands to Hal's face. "This is the elixir. You have too much inside you, and you're burning up."

Hal was wheezing now, still fumbling with his pants. He couldn't speak at all—just thinking was hard enough. Sex, he needed sex right now, even if he just jerked off. But his hands were feeling thick, as if they, too, were erect. The intense, pounding pleasure that had been lifting him up shifted, turning instead to pain. He gurgled incoherently as another wave hit him, twisting him, pushing him out further against his skin, and he fell back against the bed.

"Hal—hold on!" Morgan fell forward with him. "Hold on, Hal!"

Hal couldn't answer. He couldn't move. He hurt like he had never hurt in his life. He stared up at Morgan, mute, drowning in pain, and then, eventually, he fell under.

And then, slowly, he came back.

Hal didn't know where he'd gone, or how long he'd been there. All he knew was that he hurt like hell, but then the pain began to flow away, transformed into quiet, delicious pleasure, like a glass of very good scotch with jazz in the background. His body, instead of throbbing with pain, was humming with pleasure.

His dick, in particular, was feeling very, very good.

It felt wet and slick and—he groaned and reached down toward it, feeling as if his hand were moving through water. Someone was giving him a blow job. An *incredible* blow job. The best fucking blow job of his life. He'd only ever had two: one from a woman, and that had been awkward as hell; and one through a glory hole in Kansas City. While the latter had been good, he'd been so consumed afterward with shame that he couldn't think of it without feeling like he should rush to a confessional. But this—God help him, *this* was what a blow job should be. Hal's fumbling hand finally found his groin, and sure enough, he felt a head full of short, unruly hair. The head was bobbing in a sensual dance which, admittedly, he had not enjoyed in awhile but had not forgotten.

Hal moaned again and slid his fingers into that hair.

The head pushed abruptly against his hand and lifted up, and Hal heard a familiar voice gasp and then say, "It worked." There was a small laugh that could have doubled as a sob. "It *worked.*"

Morgan, Hal thought, blearily. The bar, the confusion: all of it came back in a rush. The drugged complacency of his earlier erotic high was gone, and he felt only awkward and afraid—afraid of Morgan, of his situation, and of himself and the arousal that he could not seem to control. He tried to withdraw, and immediately the pain came back in a rush, and he felt the blackness creeping over him again. And then, just as quickly, it receded, and he felt the pleasurable wet once more.

"Don't," Morgan said, lifting his head from Hal's groin just briefly enough to speak when Hal tried to dislodge him again. "I can't stop," he whispered and then went down on Hal again for a few seconds before speaking again. "You were nearly dead. If I stop now, you will be." He resumed his blow job then and spoke no more.

This is so fucking weird, Hal thought, but he was too weak to push Morgan away again. Also, he was starting to feel calmer, though he wasn't sure why. *It's the drug*, he realized. *It does something to relax me.* It took the shame and the fear away. It made all this somehow okay.

Hal threaded his fingers into Morgan's hair, shut his eyes, and surrendered himself to the experience.

"I'm sorry," Morgan said at another pause. "But I think things will even out for you in a moment." He lingered at the tip of Hal's cock and gave the head a swirl with his tongue before descending again.

Hal shuddered—from the release of pain, from pleasure, or from the sheer insanity of it all, he wasn't sure. There was a confused fountain of emotions inside him: shame, rage, and terror.

Yet it mixed with the hedonism of being stroked and pleasured with a hot, wet mouth—with Morgan's mouth. He found, in the end, that he could only lie there and let it happen. Despite his compliance, after a few minutes Hal felt the darkness descending again and, with it, the pain. His arms twitched and then his legs, and then he started to shake.

"Shh," Morgan whispered against the tip of his penis. "Hush. It's all right." Cool hands took Hal's balls gently, expertly massaged them, rolled them, and occasionally bent down to kiss them and take them into his mouth before returning to the shaft.

Morgan took Hal deep into his throat, and he suckled so hard Hal swore he felt it in his teeth. He felt Morgan's saliva running down between his thighs, over his scrotum, down his perineum, and he groaned because it felt good. But when he felt Morgan's fingers sliding down toward his anus, he tensed.

This. This he'd never, ever done.

"Hush," Morgan whispered again and began to tease against his entrance, working his spit against the ring.

"N-n-n-gh," Hal garbled, the closest he could come to "No." He pushed at Morgan's head again.

Morgan broke the suction on Hal's cock again, breathing very hard now. "Trust me," he whispered, and pressed harder against Hal's anus. "I don't have time to explain, but what you need to know is that you have to come. You *have* to." He pushed the tip of one finger in, and Hal cried out. "Relax," Morgan said and sucked hard against his cock again, pushing in further.

Hal tried really hard now to push him off. He groaned, and not from pleasure, because what Morgan was doing to his ass fucking hurt. Morgan pressed deeper, and Hal cried out.

"Relax," Morgan said, working slowly but relentlessly. He ran his tongue over the tip of Hal's cock again, distracting Hal as he turned his finger inside his ass, burrowing. "I'm sorry," he whispered, laving Hal's cock with his tongue between words. "I'm sorry. I didn't know. I should have. I don't know why I didn't." He pushed deeper again, and this time Hal made a rough, guttural sound that rumbled in his gut.

Know what? Hal wondered. Then Morgan's finger crooked, and Hal opened his eyes.

Wide.

Then he shut them again, moaned, and began moving his hips against the rhythm of Morgan's hand.

Yes, it had hurt at first, but it didn't now, and whatever Morgan had found to tickle inside of him was making his eyes water and the inside of his skull tingle. *Prostate*, some distant memory suggested. *That's your prostate, feeling so good.* Hal gasped. Part of his brain was sounding the alarm, shouting, *no, this isn't right!*, but the rest of him didn't care about that, really, so long as it kept making him feel so good. He stopped trying to push Morgan away and started kneading weakly against his hair. Then he gave up and simply arched and humped, pushing against that finger, against that mouth, moaning and gasping. He felt the edges of an orgasm like nothing he'd ever felt before teasing him, running through his fingers every time he came close. Sweat ran down his face and beaded on his arms, his chest, and ran down between his thighs, adding increased lubrication for Morgan's probing finger. Except it wasn't probing now. It was fucking him.

There might even have been two of them.

Morgan lifted his head and kissed the inside of Hal's thigh. "Push into it," he whispered. Hal looked down and saw Morgan's dark eyes looking up at him, and he moaned and pushed. He felt himself open, taking Morgan's fingers in deeper, and then, all of a sudden, he was coming.

He bucked and shouted and made noise like he had never done before in his life. He came in a hot, angry streak, and it went into Morgan's mouth, all of it. Morgan drank it down while he kept massaging inside Hal, milking him until he was done. Then Morgan let go, laid his head on Hal's thigh, and collapsed. His fingers, however, remained inside Hal, and after a few minutes, he turned them gently, an internal caress, and kissed the inside of Hal's thigh.

"Wha—" Hal said, then he stopped and swallowed several times, trying to wet his mouth. "What the fuck was that?"

"An orgasm," Morgan said quietly. His tongue flicked out over Hal's skin. "A very, very nice one."

No shit, Hal thought. He felt Morgan's tongue against his skin again, and he twitched. And to his surprise, so did his cock. It was still hard, in that post-orgasm stiffness that took a moment to fade, except as Morgan's mouth continued to tease his thigh, he felt the stiffness linger, then against all reason, begin to grow again.

"It's all right," Morgan murmured when Hal gasped. He was still kissing and licking Hal's thigh, and his fingers were stroking more regularly now. "I should have thought that this might happen, and I'm sorry, but you're all right now. Almost. You're more evenly balanced, but you still have the drug inside you." He nuzzled the juncture of Hal's thighs, his exhale warming Hal's already tender balls. "And now, so do I."

It took Hal a moment to process this, but then he remembered that Morgan's mouth had been latched onto his cock as he'd come, and then he remembered what Morgan had said the drug did to him. *It made him more interesting.* Hal felt Morgan's lips against his hair, his tongue against his balls. He stiffened when he felt the wet, soft touch against the skin around his anus—his full anus, still stuffed with Morgan's fingers. Morgan lifted his head, and Hal looked down at him, afraid, questioning.

"I can change," Morgan said quietly. His voice was softer, more musical, and full of heat. The very sound of it made Hal grow harder. Morgan glanced down and observed this, then smiled. "While I am taking the elixir, I can be anything." He bent down and flicked his tongue against the tip of Hal's penis, closing his lips over it briefly as his fingers probed gently inside of Hal. He smiled, seductively. "I am yours now. What do you want me to be?"

Hal was having a hard time focusing. "I don't know." He let his legs fall a little further apart, then shut his eyes and bit his lip as Morgan's fingers grew a little bolder. "I don't know."

Morgan chuckled and then bent down, kissing his way along Hal's leg, heading back toward his cock. "Come, tell me: what do you want, Howard?" he urged in a whisper. "This is your fantasy. Tell me. Whatever you want, I can do it." Hal felt a strange shimmer, and then he heard Morgan's voice higher. Still sultry, but different. "I already know you want a woman," he said, except now there was no question that *he* sounded like *she*.

Hal opened his eyes.

It was as if someone entirely different were leaning over him now—Morgan was a woman, a beautiful, *amazing,* stunning woman. Blond. Busty. Fully made up. She looked like some sort of cross between Marilyn Monroe and Caprica Six on *Battlestar Galactica.*

And it pissed Hal off. "No," he rasped, and he pushed Morgan away.

The Marilyn-Caprica woman pouted at him and then shrugged, and Hal felt her fingers withdraw discreetly from him as well. This time he watched the change. The woman exhaled loudly, deliberately, and in that release of breath, turned into millions of tiny mirrors that floated away from where her body had been and into the air. Hal heard a sharp inhale, just as loud, and at the same time, the mirrors reformed, and there was a new woman above him. Short, dark hair. Barely any breasts but enough, and they were peeping out of her black leather vest. It was, almost, the woman Hal had thought he'd seen in Morgan in the bar, the woman the spell had made him see. But it wasn't, not quite—the eyes were wrong.

All of it was wrong, actually.

"No!" Hal said again, more forcefully.

"What do you want?" the woman asked, frustrated. Her voice was smoky. Beautiful. Perfect. *Wrong.*

"Nothing!" Hal shouted. "I don't want you to be anything but yourself."

The woman frowned at him. "But my 'self' is a man. And you want a woman." She winked at him. "It's still me, Howard. But with the elixir inside me, I can *look* like anything. It's like putting on different clothes, for me. It doesn't matter."

That should have been enough. This was Hal's permission, he knew, to get out of an awkward, strange situation—he could have sex with a woman instead of a man, he could still be aroused, and he wouldn't have to feel shame. But he couldn't do it, not now that he knew.

Hal blushed and then turned his head away. He was still hard, though, and his erection, still swollen, bobbed eagerly between them. "Whatever," he said gruffly. "Just be whatever you want."

"But I want to be what *you* want," Morgan said, his voice still feminine and now agitated. "Just tell me, please!"

Hero

"I don't *know* what I want!" Hal shot back. Then he shut his eyes and reached up to run a hand over his face. His erection was beginning to become painful again, and he shifted, trying to ease himself.

"You have to tell me," Morgan said. His voice was masculine once more but was still soft and musical. "We can't linger too long, or you'll be in danger again."

Hal said nothing, and he didn't even open his eyes.

Morgan cried out in frustration—and the next thing Hal knew, his shoulders were pinned back to the bed, and Morgan was leaning over him, shouting.

"You *have to tell me*—that's how this *works!*" He shook Hal in helpless desperation. "I can't act until I know. That's what the elixir *does* to me, Howard: it makes me pliant and eager, but it makes me *dependent.* If you don't tell me, then I can't help you!"

Hal had images in his mind, and he didn't like them. He saw the cruel people at the bar forcing Morgan to be their plaything or this mysterious Eagan making him perform for their entertainment—oh, it was cruel and wrong, and he couldn't stand even the thought that this had ever happened, let alone that it might again. *No,* he thought and then opened his mouth to say it aloud. He also opened his eyes, and when he saw Morgan, he went boneless.

Because Morgan was *beautiful.*

He had changed again, but this time Morgan was like nothing Hal had ever seen before or even dreamed of. It was no longer Morgan with short, spiky hair and a leather vest, and it was no longer a woman leaning over Hal. This was Morgan with narrower, closer-set, colorless eyes, and when Hal looked into them, he thought he could see whole worlds. His face was smooth, and it glowed as if it were luminescent. He had long black hair, so black it

79

looked like the night sky complete with stars. His lips were thin, and they looked soft and inviting. He was pale and slight, and he was naked head to toe, his skin gleaming.

He was everything. He was male, Hal saw, but it didn't matter anymore. This was the person he'd seen in his vision. This was the real Morgan. Somehow, as Hal looked at him, he knew Morgan was *everything* he had ever wanted. In that moment, Hal knew he could never want anyone else again, not like this.

Morgan blushed. "I'm sorry—you upset me so much that I reverted." He glanced down at himself, winced, then lifted his chin and composed himself as he looked Hal in the eye. "Please, Howard. Please just tell me what you want so we can continue."

"This," Hal whispered. His voice was raw and faint. "I want this."

Morgan blinked, looked at himself again, and then turned back to Hal, confused. "But this isn't *anything*," he said, gesturing dismissively at himself. "This is my *very* base form, the most unpainted—if I let go any more than this, I *am* nothing more than a house. This, Howard? This is *nothing!*"

"It's what I want," Hal said, still whispering. Then another wave took him, and he winced and reached up to hold onto Morgan's bare shoulders.

He shuddered as he felt Morgan lower himself against his skin, as he felt Morgan's half-roused penis poke against his own. He felt, too, Morgan's lips brush a brief, dry kiss against his cheek.

"I don't understand," he said quietly, "but if it's what you want, I will give it to you." Hal nodded, and Morgan kissed him again, teasing the skin of his cheek. "But—how do you want it, Hal?"

Hal didn't know. He couldn't even think. Everything was fading away, and all he knew was the pain and the sweet feel of Morgan against him. He felt another kiss on his cheek, and he melted into the bed.

"Whatever you want," he said softly. When Morgan started to protest, Hal fumbled against his face until he could press numb fingers against Morgan's lips. "That's what I want," he repeated. "What I want is for you to do what *you* want." He felt the edge of the precipice and then let go and went over. "Whatever it is that you want to do to me, that's what I want."

Morgan's hand skimmed over Hal's stomach. It was shaking, and as Morgan touched him, Hal shook too. God in heaven, he was *so beautiful.*

"Whatever *I* want?" Morgan whispered.

Hal swallowed. "Unless you don't…?"

Morgan laughed, a darkly musical sound. "Oh, I want to do many, many things to you."

"Then do them," Hal said, feeling almost relieved.

Morgan took Hal's face in his hand and turned it toward him. Hal found himself staring into the strange, gray depths of the universe that was Morgan's eyes.

"This is what you want?" Morgan asked, as if he couldn't quite process this. "You want me to do to you whatever I want? *You* want to be *my* slave?"

His phrasing made Hal hesitate, but then another wave hit him, and he could only nod. "Please," he whispered, clutching at Morgan. He was almost insensate now with need and pain. "Please—*please.*"

Morgan took Hal's chin in his hand, pulled his face up, and kissed him. He kissed him hard and deep; his tongue snaked so far into Hal's mouth that it seemed to go down his throat, tickling his insides, reaching down to his groin from the inside. Hal moaned and yielded.

Morgan pulled back, breathless. "You are sincere," he said, sounding amazed. Then his face fell again. "Of course, maybe you're giving me control to keep from having to admit you want this?" Hal couldn't answer, only trembled as Morgan stroked his face. "So you understand, since this is what you have requested, you cannot take it back. You will have to endure whatever it is I wish of you. *Whatever* I wish. And I, by your command, will be compelled to execute it."

Hal felt a shiver of terror and of anticipation. But he still couldn't say anything. He didn't know whether it was the elixir taking him over again, or if it was part of the game of giving up control, or if it was what Morgan said, that he just didn't want to admit he wanted this. The latter might, he knew, be possible. But he couldn't know anything now, not for sure. Just that he wanted to let go. Really, really let go. With Morgan.

He sighed, a ragged effort, and turned his face into Morgan's neck. Lifting his chin, Morgan kissed him again briefly and then slapped him not too gently on his hip.

"Turn over onto your stomach," he said, his voice dark and slippery. "And spread your legs."

Hal moved as if in a dream, no longer thinking, not even feeling. He was bound, somehow, to the sound of Morgan's voice. He was still there, but he was fading into the spell the elixir cast and now into the release of Morgan's commands. This was no game. This was no yielding to desire in the night, no guilty sneaking to a glory hole or a forbidden glance across a bar. This was going to be the real thing. Sex. With a man.

With Morgan.

Hal lay down on the mattress, turned his face to the side, opened his legs, and waited for whatever was about to happen to begin.

He didn't feel any guilt. Not any at all. Only quiet, anxious, and glorious anticipation.

FOR several seconds nothing happened. Hal remained still, in position, his heart pounding, his will feeling as if it had been set just out of his reach. His erection was still tightening, almost painfully now, but even as he started to black out again, he found he couldn't move. He could only hold himself rigid as he slid back into darkness.

He came back slowly, feeling as if he were floating on water. He was still heavy, but he was humming too—his blood, his body, every nerve he had. Then he realized he was *literally* humming. The sound he was making was a low, guttural moan, but it felt like an atonal song. He felt *amazing*. He didn't hurt; he just felt good, really, really good.

He felt... wet.

Slowly, he began to orient himself. He was still on the bed, on his stomach, his face pressed into blankets. He clutched at them, moaning and humming, and after a moment, he humped his hips absently in pleasure. It was his ass, he realized, with dizzy shock. His ass was wet. His ass felt fucking *amazing*. He felt hands on his cheeks, spreading him for whatever was making him wet. He heard something—soft and quiet squishes, like someone lapping.

Oh Christ, Morgan was licking his ass.

He shuddered and tried to move, to shake him off, but he couldn't. *Oh God,* but that felt so good. He couldn't tell exactly what Morgan was doing, but it was… shit, it was… it was like Morgan's tongue was electric. It was everywhere and sometimes, Hal thought, trembling, he was *inside.*

He moaned again and clutched at the blankets. He should stop this. He should be ashamed; he knew that distantly. This—he'd heard of this, but he'd never *dreamed!* It was too dirty! He trembled and shut his eyes tight, and he told himself firmly, *Get away. Stop this.* But he couldn't stop this. He tried to move, but he couldn't.

New terror took him. Was *this* the spell? Was this what Morgan had meant? Morgan would do whatever he wanted, and Hal couldn't move? He gasped and clutched at the bed, feeling cold. Then abruptly, Morgan's tongue pushed deeper, and this time Hal's gasp was different. To his horror, Hal felt himself pushing back.

Was *that* the spell? Or had *he* done that because it felt so fucking good?

Hal didn't know. He was so confused now. He didn't have a clue why he was doing anything anymore. He had never felt so vulnerable or exposed. Old terrors surfaced, the same ghosts that made him jump even in his bedroom if there was a noise in the apartment while he was jerking off to a magazine. Someone, somehow, would eventually catch him, and then—then he didn't know, but it wouldn't be good. He couldn't imagine what would happen if anyone found him letting *this* happen, no matter how wonderful it was.

You're in a room with no doors and no windows, a voice inside his head reminded him. *It's just you here with Morgan. You're safe, Hal. Here, with him, you're safe.*

For some reason this only made Hal more tense. He shut his eyes even tighter and cut off another moan. "Morgan," he whispered, terrified. "*Morgan!*"

Morgan lifted his head, just for a moment. "Get on your knees," he ordered and then went back to work.

He'd put his face back into Hal's ass, but he helped Hal heft first one leg, then the other. When Hal tried to lift his head, Morgan pushed it back down.

"No. Stay down. Just relax," he said.

"Morgan," Hal whispered again. "Morgan—"

"Let go," Morgan ordered him. His tongue laved Hal, swirling slowly toward its target. "Let go, Howard. Let go to me."

Hal braced himself on his forearms, feeling exposed and strange and uncomfortable as Morgan nudged his hips wider, still licking and sometimes—Hal shuddered—*sucking*. He was using his fingers now, too, tugging on Hal's cock, his balls, stroking his perineum, and then, to Hal's terror and delight, pressing into him again. Hal shut his eyes tighter, huffed, and then, remembering what Morgan had said earlier, forced himself to relax.

Let go. Just let go. Let go.

Morgan's fingers slid deep inside him, and Hal opened himself further, whimpering as Morgan's finger found his prostate again.

He felt a soft, wet kiss against his ass cheek. "You are so hot," Morgan said, his voice low and sultry. "You have no idea how hot you look right now." Morgan kissed him again, his tongue stealing out to lick the crack between his cheeks. "You're beautiful, and you're wonderful. And I want to give you nothing but pleasure, Howard. Nothing but absolutely perfect pleasure."

Hal couldn't speak, so he just lay there, exposed, vulnerable, and completely at Morgan's mercy. He had never been like this, not even close. Morgan was pushing very deeply now, brushing so regularly against his prostate that Hal's mouth was hanging open, making him drool into the blanket. Morgan was trailing kisses over his backside, his lower back, the rim of his anus—oh God, it felt so, so good.

So good, so good, so good, so good.

"Keep making noise," Morgan said, his voice raw and breathless. He still spoke softly, but there was a command inside the tone that crawled inside Hal's spine and made him turn into pudding. Morgan bent and placed a sucking kiss on each of Hal's shoulder blades. "I like it when you make noise."

And because he could not refuse him, Hal began to moan again, regularly now. He moaned, and he gasped, and he grunted, sometimes mumbling incoherently, begging Morgan not to stop, to do that, yeah, *just like that, oh God, harder, harder, harder,* until he was lost in his own speech, murmuring in an erotic tongue. *Let go,* the voice inside his head urged him. His own voice, Morgan's—he didn't know, and he didn't need to know. *Let go. Let go, let go, let go.*

And he did.

Hal surrendered, not even letting himself discover if it was his will and his desire or if this was something Morgan had done. It didn't matter how it had happened. It was happening, and it was good. It was the dirtiest, most carnal, most *wonderful* thing that had ever happened to him—ever. Why had he waited so long for this? Why had he told himself he was too old, that no one would want him now, that he just didn't like the gay men he saw at clubs—why had he made so many excuses, if *this* was what sex, real sex was like? Except, even as he thought this, he knew that somehow this was different because this was with Morgan. He'd fumbled with men in the dark, but they'd felt wrong too. Everyone was wrong for him, somehow.

Everyone but Morgan.

Hal gasped as he felt a push, then pressure, and then a low, deep fire as something filled him, and he realized that something else was in his ass. Morgan. Morgan was inside him. *Oh God, yes,* he thought, and then he let himself go even further, surrendering again. He gasped, then shuddered, and then held on as Morgan started to move.

It was a quick, efficient fucking—and rough, the sort of stuff that made Hal too nervous to watch even on the Internet. But now he was living it, and it was wonderful. It was animal, it was carnal, and it was, in its own way, very beautiful. Morgan moved hard and fast, like a piston driving more and more sound out of Hal until he was simply shouting, a long, deep cry punctuated by Morgan's thrusts. Hal felt himself starting to come and braced for it, but at the last second Morgan pulled out. Like lightning, he flipped Hal over with surprising strength, and Morgan fell onto Hal's cock like a starving man, sucking and stroking him back into his orgasm, which he drank down greedily and completely. Hal was so spent he couldn't keep his eyes open to watch; he caught one image of his lover's dark head going down, and then he could only lay back and gasp for air, feeling the tickle of Morgan's long black hair as he finished. But when he felt Morgan's mouth sliding up his sternum, he forced his eyes to open, watching as Morgan appeared before him, bracing himself over Hal on the bed.

"You would think," Morgan said, breathless but not quite as spent as Hal, "that your command would free me, but it's funny how it actually binds me even more. Until the elixir is passed from my system, I must succumb to my every desire regarding you. And there is so, so much I want to do to you." His eyes went dark, like a storm, and he reached out to stroke Hal's cheek. "But the interesting thing is that, unlike when Eagan binds me, I feel recharged with you. Each draught of you, elixir-charged, only makes me stronger. You are like light, Howard. My own shining light."

"Stronger," Hal repeated, basking quietly in the praise. *I am his light.* "Have I made you strong enough to free you?"

Morgan smiled sadly. "Nothing can free me." He stroked Hal's neck and his eyes went even darker, losing their irises entirely. "But I can do a few other interesting things with what you've done for me. Some of which I think you will particularly enjoy."

He bent and kissed Hal deeply, and Hal shuddered because he thought Morgan's tongue was changing inside his mouth, swelling, shrinking, and once, he'd thought, splitting and wrapping around his own. Morgan nudged his legs, and Hal pulled them up higher, gasping into Morgan's mouth as he slid back inside. Morgan went deeper than he'd been before, spreading Hal, filling him, and doing strange things inside him that he couldn't even visualize, let alone describe. Hal tipped his head back and began to convulse as he swore he felt Morgan's cock snaking inside him, moving farther inside him than was anatomically possible.

Morgan was suckling his neck. His hips were barely moving, but they hardly needed to. "Hold still," he murmured, dragging his mouth down to Hal's nipple. "Hold very, very still."

Hal cried out, his voice going high, his eyes opening wide but unseeing as he felt Morgan spread out into his veins—up, up so high he was inside Hal's spine, and then Morgan went all the way up to the top of his head.

Then he pushed. And Hal exploded.

He shattered: he felt himself break; he saw stars; he felt all the million, trillion pieces he had become; he felt himself die. And then, in a rush like breath, he felt himself come back down.

And then, like a surreal afterthought, he came. Again.

He bucked against Morgan, shouting—but weakly, because he was still fuzzy from the explosion. Then he felt his semen shoot warm and thick from his body, hitting Morgan's belly, dripping down onto his own chest.

He found his breath and then lifted his head and reached weakly for Morgan's hair.

Morgan smiled, his eyes still shining like liquid silver. "So, you *did* like it," he said.

In answer, Hal hauled his face back up and kissed him, wet and open-mouthed and pliant. He noticed, as they parted, that no matter what position Morgan's head was in, his cock was always inside of Hal. *Shape-shifter.*

"You didn't come," he said, a little stunned.

Morgan shook his head. "I can't."

"Why not?" Hal asked.

"Partly because that is something Eagan doesn't want, and he wants it with enough emphasis that I can't easily break it. But the other reason is because you're human. No one knows what will happen if I have an orgasm with a human." Morgan traced a finger down Hal's collarbone. "I don't shoot semen like you do, Howard. I... flood."

"Like, you make a lot of it?" Hal asked, thinking of mess. And not really minding.

Morgan shook his head. "No. *I* flood. My... spirit, I guess you could say, but that isn't right. I don't have a form when I climax. When I came to sexual maturity and I masturbated the first time, you can imagine my shock when I discovered it took me into what felt like an alternate universe. I found my way back, which took some doing the first time, but for a long, long time, I never did it with anyone else. And when I did, I found that it took my lover's spirit along with me. If I come, Howard, *I* come inside you." He spread his hand over Hal's chest, and up his neck. "You would feel me everywhere."

"I sort of did," Hal said. "Before—when you... did that thing. That—that was good."

"This is even more," Morgan said. His hand slid down to play with Hal's penis, which was starting to get hard again. "It's like that but then further. It's very sensual and beautiful and intense. But." His hand slid down, teasing where their bodies were joined. "There's a risk."

"Of what?" Hal asked, trying to imagine something even more intense than the shattering he'd felt before.

"Death," Morgan said.

Hal paused. "Yours or mine?"

Morgan shrugged, though he couldn't hide his nervousness. "It's one of those things where there's a chance for something truly amazing, but the cost is that it might be horrible instead. I don't know how it works, exactly, but it has to do with molecules and physics. And biorhythms—yours and mine. If it works, we sort of align, and everything changes. Technically, we would rewrite the universe just a little. Bungee jumping through physics. You would, in this analogy, be the cord. You're the resistance."

Hal was starting to get it. "But maybe I snap in half?"

"Or I lose hold of the cord. Or we slam into the side of the building or the water or the support beam of the bridge. Or we have the most amazing ride. Or we bring down half the world around our ears. Or worse." He sighed and then traced a line across Hal's chest. "Sweet Howard. How I wish you truly were my hero, that you could stay forever."

"I thought you said I couldn't leave," Hal said.

Morgan shook his head. "I won't let them hurt you. I'll find a way to get you out."

"And what about you?" Hal asked. "How will you get out?"

Morgan arched an eyebrow at him, trying to look amused, but Hal saw the pain behind the look. "What do you care about what happens to me, Howard Porter?"

I care about you. I care about you a lot. Hal blushed and then set his jaw and said gruffly, "It isn't right."

"Many things in this world aren't right," Morgan replied quietly, sadly. He leaned forward and nipped at Hal's ear. "Now shut your mouth, Howard, because I'm going to fuck you again."

And fuck they did. They fucked in every single way possible. For hours.

Technically, it was Hal who was fucked. He would have been more than willing to reciprocate, to try out both ends of guiltless sex, but Morgan gave him no chance. For a long time they had been half-dressed, but now they were naked, writhing, sliding over one another, rolling in the sheets. And all the while, Morgan was inside Hal. He drove hard, taking Hal from the front, from the side, from behind, once even bending forward and biting, very hard, into the meat of Hal's shoulder. He told Hal what position he wanted, and Hal obeyed, going onto his knees, letting Morgan mount him, letting himself be pressed against the wall, leaning over the edge of the bed, hanging upside down and pushing up into him, fucking himself on Morgan's cock—and always, always moaning for him, telling him in increasingly incoherent tones how the fucking made him feel.

Morgan was thoughtful, too, adding strange lotions to their play when the onslaught began to make Hal sore, working them inside Hal and stimulating him at the same time. He made Hal hold himself open while he did it, letting Hal know he was still the subordinate, face down, his hot breath steaming his own chest as he watched his swollen sex bob as Morgan manipulated Hal's cock from inside. He never denigrated Hal, and he barely spoke, but that only increased the excitement as the large, muscled construction worker knelt and exposed himself for the slight, beautiful, shape-shifter.

After the fifth time that Hal came, he stayed flaccid for a while and his erection took a long time to return. Morgan let him rest then, and Hal watched, aroused only in mind as Morgan lapped Hal's semen from the pool it had made on his stomach. He had done this every time, either swallowing it or finding it after. It gave him more of the drug, he said, plus it helped him gauge how much remained. Hal found it erotic. He opened his mouth to tell him so, but before he could, Morgan finished and slid up to lie beside him. Hal didn't mind that he still tasted a little of himself on Morgan's tongue.

"Is it over?" Hal asked, letting his hand rest against Morgan's sweat-slick chest. "Is it out of me?"

"Almost," he said, breathless. His arms were draped over Hal's hip, his long fingers stealing back to run over the tender line of Hal's backside. He watched Hal's eyes, his own still dark and pulsing from the drug. "How are you doing? Too sore?"

"I'm okay," Hal said. He probably wouldn't be able to sit down for a day, but he wasn't thinking about that much just now.

Morgan's finger was running slow circles over Hal's tender flesh, teasing at times, near his anus but never touching it. "So," he said, suddenly hesitant again. "You seem… to be enjoying this."

Hal tried to sort out how to answer this one. His fingers traced the line of Morgan's nipple. "Yes," he said simply.

Morgan said nothing more, just held still as Hal continued to play. He shivered and then gasped quietly as Hal bent and took the nipple into his mouth. "*Oh.* That's very nice."

"Nice?" Hal murmured and suckled hard, drawing the nipple completely into his mouth as well as some flesh.

"*Yes.*" Morgan gasped again and clutched at Hal's shoulders. His voice was breathy now, and he was arching against Hal's mouth, which had formed a seal around the nipple as his tongue flicked against the flesh inside his mouth. Morgan clutched at his head, digging his fingers into Hal's hair. Hal broke away, taking in air, nuzzling his way to the other nipple. Hal looked up at him, liking the way Morgan's face softened. Then, abruptly, Morgan was sad again.

Hal lifted his face. "What is it?"

Morgan shook his head. "Nothing." He bent down and kissed Hal, and Hal reached up and pinched the nipple he had been suckling a few moments ago.

Morgan slid a leg between Hal's, nudging him open as he shifted his body, hovering close to Hal's hand as he pressed his pelvis against Hal's hip, his hard penis nudging against Hal's stomach. He didn't try to make love to him but just lay there, watching him as if he were memorizing his face and enjoying the experience.

Hal looked back at him, doing the same, and then thought abruptly, *I love him.*

The revelation made him startle and then blush. Morgan raised an eyebrow.

"Is something wrong?" he asked.

Hal only blushed harder. Wrong! Yes, there was something wrong! What kind of idiot was he? *Love him!* He'd known him what, three hours? But then he looked up at him again, and the feeling came back, even stronger. He did love him. He *loved* Morgan. He loved him in his gut, in the soles of his shoes. He loved him ridiculously, for no reason that made sense or ever would. He just loved him. That was all. It was a wild, strange, and terrifying realization.

And even worse, he knew that he had to tell him.

But he couldn't make the words come out. He *tried.* But the fear choked him, the old terrors, and they beat at him, warning him that Morgan would laugh or be appalled. *Don't start with that, you idiot!* they shouted. *He doesn't even know you're gay! Don't tell him that you love him!*

Morgan was watching him carefully, curious but not yet concerned. He was stroking Hal's face and looking so sweet and tender that Hal thought, if he spoke very quickly, maybe he could at least manage a gurgled confession. But before he could speak, Morgan did.

"I wish I could come inside you," he said quietly. Longingly. He was still stroking Hal, and he paused to tuck a hair behind his ear. "I wish you truly were my hero, my magic prince come to take me away from all this. I wish I could surrender to you without a drug, without the desperation of saving your life. I wish you truly could set me free." Now *he* was blushing, but just a little. Mostly he just looked sad. "I know you won't like this, what we've done together, when it's over. But it's enough, I think, maybe, that it was this good. Because it was, Howard. I hope it was good for you, even

94

if you dislike it later. I hope, for this moment, you enjoyed being with me as much as I enjoyed being with you."

Hal's throat was thick. He reached up and touched Morgan's cheek, his hand trembling. "I won't dislike this," he whispered. "Ever." Morgan gave him a wry smile, and Hal knew he didn't understand. He pushed past the fear and tried, again, to find the words. "No," he said, gruffly. "I won't—*ever*. I l—" *love you.* He shuddered. "I l-lo—"

He'll laugh, he'll laugh, he'll laugh!

Hal swallowed and then shut his eyes tight. "I like guys," he whispered pathetically.

Morgan *did* laugh, but it was light and pleasant. "I'm sorry— you what?"

"I like guys," Hal said again. He opened his eyes, hating himself for how even this mild confession made him panic. "I don't find women attractive. Only men."

Morgan frowned, looking at Hal as if he were extremely confused. "Then why did Shinju—"

"Because I lied to her," Hal said, still whispering. "Because I was afraid, and so when she asked me who I'd seen in the window, I said I saw a woman."

He felt hot and sick, and he waited for Morgan's anger, his rage—his rejection. But Morgan only laughed again in his quiet, gentle way and drew Hal closer to kiss his cheek.

"Poor Howard!" he said, and kissed him again.

"I was so confused," Hal said in a breathless rush. *He's not angry.* Maybe he could tell him more. Maybe. *Maybe.* "I'd never been attracted to a girl before."

Morgan's kisses became nuzzles. "So you *were* attracted to me? As a man?"

"Yes," Hal confessed, breathless. *Like water to the earth. Like flowers to the sun.* He shut his eyes and nuzzled back, shaking. "I'm not—good with words."

Morgan's hands were sliding over him again. When he spoke, his voice was low and sultry, and it purred. "We don't need words, Howard. Not even one."

Three, Hal thought guiltily again as Morgan pressed him back into the bed once more. *I need to give you three.*

But he didn't. He felt them burning at the back of his throat, pounding in his chest, wrapping around them as Morgan made slow, beautiful love to him, the sort of lovemaking that you see in movies and know is too beautiful to be real, the sort you imagine in your dreams, the sort that takes you, effortlessly, straight to the stars. All that time the words screamed inside him, desperate to get out, and Hal felt their urgency claw away at his fear. He had to tell him. He had to take the risk, *had* to tell him, and he had to tell him *now.* But he couldn't, not even when he came, shouting out his release as Morgan pushed him once more over the edge. He could only fall back, spent, empty, and silent.

"Sleep," Morgan whispered, staying inside him as he reached up to stroke Hal's face. "Sleep, darling Howard. The poison is gone. You're free. Just sleep and it will all be better."

I'll tell him when I wake up, Hal thought dizzily, because sleep did sound good just then. He grunted incoherently and reached up to stroke Morgan's shoulder and then dragged him back down against his chest again.

Morgan's face was buried in his neck, his breath coming hard against Hal's collarbone, and Hal reached up with a heavy, drunken hand to pat him. Morgan put his hand on Hal's shoulder and nuzzled his jaw lightly.

"Thank you," he whispered. "That was the best time I've ever had." He kissed Hal's temple gently. "I will never forget you. Ever."

Hal was starting to feel very, very fuzzy. He tried to tell Morgan he wasn't going anywhere, that he just needed to rest for a moment, but he couldn't speak. *Sleep,* he urged himself. He'd just sleep, just for a moment, and then he'd take a few minutes to sort this out in his head. Then, when he was rested and organized, he'd tell him. Well, maybe, just to be old-fashioned, first he'd sit down and talk with him, to learn more about what the hell being the Oasis meant, to find out about this Eagan bastard, and to try and convince Morgan to leave or to kick that guy out. He would get to know him, and *then* he'd tell him he loved him, but not just now. Right now he was so tired, so spent, that all he could do was slide, like water through a pipe, into sleep.

He went, and he dreamt of nothing at all. He felt warm and safe and happy. Very, very happy. And content. *Love.* He was surrounded and protected by love.

But when Hal woke up, when he opened his eyes, he knew right away that something was wrong.

The smell caught him first. He didn't smell Morgan's spicy, earthy scent, just dust and deadness. When he opened his eyes, he didn't see Morgan's carefully gathered collection of treasures or his curtains or anything—all he saw was the sagging bare mattress he was sitting on and the bare olive walls and the rows of empty metal shelves. He was naked and he was sore. His clothes were lying in a neat pile beside him.

Morgan was nowhere in the room. And the room, suddenly, had a door.

Hal studied it warily for several seconds. Then he glanced around the room again. "Morgan?" he called, but there was, of course, no answer because there was nothing in this room but him.

Hal dressed hurriedly and approached the door. When he turned the knob, it opened and the door swung soundlessly into an empty hall. Hal moved into it cautiously, ready for some *laumu* to come and try to attack. But it was the same as the room, dull and empty. Morgan wasn't here, either. *No one* was here. And when Hal took a step forward, calling for Morgan again, the door shut behind him. When Hal turned toward it, he saw that the door was gone. A blank wall stood in its place.

"Morgan?" He started toward the stairs. "Morgan? *Morgan?*"

He hurried down the hall, searching, shouting, but there were no more doors, only stairs at the end and a window. When he went down the stairs, they vanished behind him, turning into a wall.

He ran through the empty bar, but it looked as if no one had been there in ten years. Hal opened a door that he thought would lead him into another hallway, but it took him outside, and when he stepped through the archway, the wall filled in behind him.

When he let go of the door, it swung shut, and the whole building vanished.

Hal stood there, stunned, confused, and as realization dawned on him, aching.

And furious.

"Morgan!"

Hal was standing at the corner across from the building site, which was quiet and empty in the early morning. Behind him was a vacant lot, barren and sorry and empty, looking very much as if nothing had ever been there, certainly not mere moments ago.

Hero

There was no sign of Morgan, the bar, or anything.

"*Morgan!*" he shouted again. "Morgan! Morgan!" And then, swallowing his fear, he added, almost as loudly, "I love you!"

But there was no answer: no laugh, no recoil, no nothing, because there was no one here to hear them. The Oasis—and Morgan—were gone.

CHAPTER 5
Kitsune

HAL wandered around the empty lot and the surrounding area for hours, looking for the bar, for Morgan, for Shinju, or for anything at all. But it was as if none of it had happened. Every part of the experience had been erased so completely that he might have been able to convince himself he'd fallen asleep on a bench and dreamed the whole thing, including walking out of a building that disappeared behind him as he left it. The only trace left of his time in the Oasis was in his mouth, where the taste of Morgan still lingered, and in his body, where the feel of him still remained.

But this was all, and these whispers gave Hal no clue how to find Morgan again. He tried for hours, wandering everywhere and sometimes calling out, but there was no one around, just the occasional street bum or group of kids. A few times he thought he saw a shadow lengthening across the empty lot, but if he moved toward it, it vanished. There was no sign of Morgan or the Oasis anywhere. The only life at all was at the convenience store around the corner, with only the clerk and a gruff-looking customer inside.

After several hours, Hal went back to the store and used the pay phone to call a cab. He bought a prepackaged sandwich and a bottle of water and consumed both absently while he waited. He rode in silence all the way to his apartment, watching out the windows, his eyes scanning the sides of the road, knowing all the while that he wasn't going to find anything. When he was home, he paid the driver, went upstairs, and let himself in.

He sat for a long time at his kitchen table, staring at an open bottle of beer that he never drank. He felt a strange tightness in his chest, alternating with a hollowness that was like nothing he'd ever felt. He wasn't hungry. He wasn't thirsty. He wasn't anything.

Just sad. He felt heavy and lost and very, very sad.

After a while, he felt something warm inside his pocket; when he reached in, he found the coin that had been his St. Thomas medal glowing softly, still bearing the image of the fox. He swallowed another wave of sorrow, pocketed the coin, stood wearily, and then went to the bathroom. He used the toilet, took a shower, and fell onto his bed, naked and clutching the coin.

He fell asleep immediately, and he dreamed he was running through the stars, chasing a woman who turned into a fox with nine tails, but he never found her. When he woke, it was dark, and his chest hurt. He touched his face and was surprised to find that his eyes were swollen and that his cheeks and pillow were wet with his tears. He got dressed, ate a can of soup without tasting it, and then, though he didn't know why, grabbed his keys, and left.

The city was humming quietly around him as he pulled his car out of the lot and onto the freeway. Traffic, as usual, was abysmal, but Hal barely noticed. He didn't even turn on his radio. He just drove, not really knowing where he was going, until he found himself, unsurprisingly, back at the empty lot beside the construction site. He parked illegally and then sat on the curb beside his car and stared at the place where the bar had been. In the dark of night, it was little more than a gaping black hole.

There were shapes moving in the darkness, strange things that, like the bar, appeared to be there only to vanish as soon as Hal blinked or looked away. There were large, ominous shapes, moving slowly like zombies through fog, and there were smaller, scuttling shapes. They made Hal uneasy and frightened him, but they didn't scare him away. He stayed there, actually hoping that one of them would catch him and take him back to the Oasis and to Morgan. But even though the empty lot was crawling with the ghosts, none of them came within twenty feet of him, and after a while they faded entirely. The only thing Hal saw now was a dog walking down the side street—a big, white dog with pointed ears, like a German shepherd. It wasn't a ghost and it wasn't magical. The only thing interesting about it at all was that either its tail was moving very fast or it had too many.

Except, Hal thought as he continued to watch it, it wasn't a German shepherd. He rose to his feet, his heart starting to beat faster. Actually, it wasn't even a dog.

It looked more like a fox.

The fox glanced over its shoulder, saw Hal, and ran. And Hal ran after it.

He bounded down the street, beyond the lights and into the darkness, not even considering for a second that it was a very stupid thing to do after hours in a dead section of Los Angeles. He wouldn't have stopped even if that had occurred to him. It was just like his dream. Except this time, he was going to catch her.

Hal ran and ran until his chest was fit to burst, and then he kept running anyway, ignoring the now-screaming pain in his whole leg, not stopping for anything until there she was, the woman from his dream. He saw now that she was also Shinju. She was still wearing the fur coat, and she was sitting under a lamplight on a park bench, calm and composed. She looked up at Hal, unsurprised to see him, and smiled, though the gesture didn't quite reach her eyes.

"Determined, I see," she said. "Alas, it comes too late."

"I saw you," Hal rasped, still trying to catch his breath. He braced against the back of the bench to keep himself from falling over. *What do you mean, too late?* Hal wiped his mouth with the back of his hand. "I saw you in my dream. You were a fox. You had nine tails."

"I saw you as well. You shouted at me, and you wept." She narrowed her eyes at him. "Tell me, Howard Porter. What did you weep for?"

Hal tried to read her face, to tell if she was mocking him or not. He couldn't, so he glared at her. "Why did you send me in there?" he demanded, working hard to keep himself under control.

She looked him up and down with disdain, and when she spread her lips, baring her teeth to speak again, Hal could see the fox in her. "Because I thought you were someone *helpful.*"

"You made me think he was a woman!" Hal shot back. "You tricked me; you almost got me killed! And then he sent me away!" Hal waved his hands in a vague gesture of angry frustration. "What the hell is going on?!"

For a long time, she simply stared at him, haughty, cold, and beneath it all, angry. "Go back to your life, human," she said at last with disdain. "Go back and forget."

"I can't," Hal said, clenching his fists at his sides.

Her lips thinned in a smile. "Very well." She raised her chin, and her eyes began to glow. "I will *make* you forget."

Hal stepped back quickly, holding his hands up in front of his face. "No! *No!*" He shut his eyes and turned his face away, hoping that if he didn't look at her, it would be enough. He felt a wind, sharp and cold, brush across his face. *No,* he thought sadly, assuming this would be the spell, but when it passed, he found to his relief that he could still remember. He lowered his hands and saw Shinju staring at him, her expression still guarded, but he thought she looked a little gentler.

"I want to go back," Hal said. He gestured into the fog. "I want to help him." *I love him.* Hal worried that she would make him confess this, but he wouldn't let the fear take hold this time. He would say it if he had to. He *would* say it, this time.

She didn't ask him, but he wondered if she could read his mind like Morgan, because she smiled, the gesture thin and faint, and held out her hand. "Come with me, then, Howard Porter. And I will tell you a story."

Her hand, white and small, glowed as if caught in moonlight, but the moon was obscured by clouds. Hal reached out and put his hand in hers and found that it was cold. An image flashed across his mind of cherry blossoms and snow, a white fox with nine tails sitting in the branches. Then it was gone and there was only Shinju, looking amused.

"Come," she said, and led him forward into the fog.

THEY walked in gray darkness for what seemed like hours, or perhaps it was only minutes. Hal felt dizzy and disoriented, at times so much so that he forgot his own name or why he was here. He had no idea where he was and hadn't since he'd gone after the fox in the fog. But sometimes he would put his hand into the pocket of his jeans and find the coin again, and he would remember it all once more. After forgetting twice, he simply kept his fingers pressed against the metal and he was fine.

Shinju said nothing, and Hal did not dare to speak. He thought, perhaps, that they were walking through time or something else equally magical, but when the fog finally parted, he was surprised to find he was just off Hollywood Boulevard in what could only be the present day. They were standing outside a small, old-fashioned theater, its marquee unlit and empty. But a woman in a sari sat at the ticket window. When Shinju approached, the woman sold her two tickets, and she and Hal went inside.

The theater was what Hal's mother would have called "clumsy." At first glance it looked dirty and unkempt, but there was, in fact, no dirt, just age. In Kansas, Hal would have called this an old vaudeville theater, but God only knew what anything had started out as in LA. All he knew was that, once, this place had been grand, and that day had been a long, long time ago. Now it was just worn around the edges; the seats weren't uncomfortable, but they weren't any high-backed plush stadium seats, that was for sure. It was the sort of place kept up by a sole proprietor, not a chain, with an atmosphere that was quaint and nostalgic if you only came to one or two shows, but sad and tired if you had to look at it often, and depressing if you looked at it every night, especially with the house lights on while you cleaned up spilled soda and popcorn.

Shinju seated them in the third row from the back, three seats in. A movie was already playing on the screen. A beaming young Indian man in ridiculously white pants was dancing around the most obvious soundstage in the world, clasping his hands to his chest and thrusting his hips as the camera occasionally panned to an impossibly beautiful sari-clad woman standing on a balcony, looking out like a 1940s heroine at a paper moon.

"This is one of my favorites," Shinju said as they sat down. She smiled and pointed at the man on the screen. "He's a singer at a local bar. She weaves carpets and lives with her grandmother. He loves her, but she loves her grandmother's boarder, who, of course, is an ass and not worth her time."

Hal nodded, not really sure what he was supposed to say to that. He didn't give a damn about the movie. He wanted to talk about real life, about what had happened at the Oasis, about Morgan, about how he could get back. But when he turned to speak to her, she only held up a hand and motioned for him to be quiet. Hal opened his mouth to speak anyway and choked as he realized she had somehow stolen his voice. Shocked, angry, and more than a little scared, he settled back uneasily in his seat to watch the movie and wait. After a few minutes, Shinju waved a hand at him, and he felt his throat tickle. He cleared his throat and shuddered with relief to find that he could hear the sound. He said nothing more, however, and continued to watch and to wait.

Other women came on the screen, and Shinju leaned over again. "Those are the hookers," she explained.

Hal blinked. "Pretty good-looking hookers," he said, thinking of the strung-out, garish tarts lining the back streets of LA—and some of the front ones too.

"And it's a very good-looking slum." She pointed at the heroine. "What do you think—could you fall in love with her?"

Hal gave her a look that he hoped communicated *are you insane?* "I've been watching this movie for five minutes, and all they've done is sing."

"He took one look at her standing on a bridge in the rain, and he was lost. Half an hour later, all she'd done was weep and jump over puddles and refuse to tell him so much as her name, and yet he has fallen and will never rise again."

"This is a movie," Hal pointed out. "Real life isn't like that."

Shinju's smile thinned. "Yes, that's what everyone likes to say. And yet, people make snap judgments in love and everything else every day. For example, forgetting for a moment all your anger at me, would you even have considered going into the bar if I had told you that the princess you dreamed of was, in fact, actually a prince?"

Hal clenched his jaw and stared angrily at the screen. He watched the hero take the shy woman in his arms, bending her backward in a perfect arc while the "moonlight" lit up the sheer colors of her sari. After several minutes, he spoke.

"I wasn't sure what I saw," he admitted tersely.

"But you wanted Morgan to be a woman, not a man," she said, just as tightly.

Hal hesitated. That was a tough one.

"I gave you what you wanted," Shinju said. "That was what the spell did. It turned Morgan into whatever you wanted him to be."

Hal felt angry again, but this time at himself. Was he so messed up inside that he actually wanted the men he found attractive to be women so he didn't have to feel guilty? He realized, with a sickening certainty, that the answer was yes. He glowered.

"You *encouraged* me to see Morgan as a woman," he said, and turned to face her. "Those kisses you put on my eyes—they were spells, weren't they? And you did something with the coin, too, the coin that used to be my medallion." He reached into his pocket and touched it lightly and then looked expectantly at Shinju. When she only smiled, Hal grew angry. "You think this is funny?" Hal aimed a finger at the screen. "My life is not some story for you to mess around with!"

He was shouting, and people in the rows ahead of them turned around and shushed him. He ignored them, and so did Shinju, who had finally stopped smiling.

"I don't think this is funny at all," she said. "But you're wrong. Your life *is* some story, and I can 'mess around' with it because it's my story too."

The music had started gain, and now the song the hero had been singing came to a great climax. As it did, the theater lit up as starbursts exploded across the screen. It lit up Shinju's face as well, and Hal looked at her, really looked at her, at her face. Her very familiar face. It was a slightly different shape, but those eyes, that nose, that mouth—he had seen them before, hovering over him, as slim hands brought him to passion he hadn't even known to dream of.

"Mother," he whispered. "You're Morgan's mother."

Shinju gave a deep nod, her eyes falling shut as she bowed her head. Then she lifted her face to Hal's again. There was no more amusement or even blankness. Only pain.

"Yes," she said. "He is my son. And you are the only person in the world who can save him."

THEY'D left the movie after that. Now they were sitting in the back booth of an Indian restaurant down the street, but they weren't eating the food they had ordered. Neither of them seemed to know what to do now or what to say. This more than anything unsettled Hal—he realized he had grown accustomed to her bullying, teasing him with information. Her silence now seemed ominous.

Hal shoved his plate and the basket of naan away from him. "Tell me the story," he said, leaning onto the table toward her. "Tell me how all this happened."

Shinju ran her finger around the lip of her mug of tea, staring into it sadly as she spoke. "It began many years ago, when our clan first came to this country." She smiled sadly. "We were such fools. We thought, like the immigrants we traveled with, that this land would be an opportunity for freedom and autonomy. We didn't account for how many others of our kind would be here, too, and how tricky they would be."

She waved her hand, and a book appeared out of nowhere, the same one that Hal had seen his mystery novel turn into at the bus stop. It lay open on the table between them, old and worn, though it was clear it had once been a grand thing. The paper was thick, and the printing wasn't weird symbols but writing—Japanese, Hal thought, but he wasn't exactly sure—heavy and intricate, the edges gilded in what might very well have been real gold. Shinju waved her hand again and the pages turned themselves, stopping on a brightly colored illustration of a white fox sitting in the center of a midnight landscape, its nine tails fanned out behind it like a peacock.

"I am *kitsune*," she said, gesturing to the fox. "I am a shape-shifter native to Japan. I came over the ocean to see the new land where the emigrants had gone, but on the way, a spirit of the sea seduced me, and when I arrived, I gave birth to my son. I named him Sora." Shinju picked up the mug and smiled over the rim. "He was a beautiful, magical child, and I loved him simply for that, but as he grew, I realized he was not *kitsune*, nor sea spirit, but something different. Sora was not just a boy, he was a sanctuary. As he grew, what we came to call the Oasis grew up around him, a sort of bubble of a world that kept out whatever he wished to keep out and kept in those he loved."

Her smile faded. "But as he grew, he changed again, and it was then that I failed him: I failed to see the man he had become, and I failed to accept the sort of man he was. And when my failure made him vulnerable, a trickster spirit took advantage. He seduced my Sora and tricked him into casting out the *kitsune*, and now he is a prisoner inside himself. He doesn't even know his true name any longer. Sora is gone. Eagan changed him forever, and so he was renamed. Sora is dead, and Morgan is in his place. But Morgan is still the Sora of my heart. He is still my son. And I may not see my son or dwell in his heart ever again."

She looked down at her hands. "When I sent you into the Oasis, to my son, I enchanted you so that you would see what you wanted to see. I saw your heart, and I knew there was a chance that you might be able to free him, and so I tried to make your way as narrow and easy as I could so that you would not fail. I could see that you could never love a man as you would need to love Sora to free him, and so I enchanted you, so that you would see him as you needed to see him."

You manipulated me, and you used me, Hal translated silently, his jaw locking in anger. But it wouldn't hold, because he knew, too, that he had manipulated himself. His hand tightened on the table, but he forced it to relax before he spoke.

"You made me hurt him," he said.

Shinju's head jerked up, her nose wrinkling and lips curling as she snarled. "You would have rejected him if I had not enchanted you! You could not love him as a man!"

"I don't love anybody just by looking at them," Hal shot back, "no matter how many Bollywood movies you put in front of me!" He stopped and then let his shoulders fall forward slightly. "The thing is, actually, I'm... not attracted to women."

Hero

Shinju looked at him with narrowed eyes. "Then why—?"

Hal ran a hand through his hair and stared at the tabletop. "I didn't know who you were, or why you were asking." He felt himself going red. "This, actually, is the first I've ever admitted it out loud." *Except to Morgan.* The thought pained him, and he stared miserably into his half-eaten dinner. "I've always wished I could just be normal, like I know everybody wants me to be. But I'm not. I can't be." He laughed bitterly at himself. "So I guess that's why, when you enchanted me to make Morgan 'as I needed to see him,' I saw him as a woman—because I am just that fucked-up."

Shinju was silent, and when Hal finally got the courage to look up at her, she looked a little strange. Her eyes were a little damp, but she was stiff and hesitant as she spoke. "You can never be normal, Howard Porter," she said very quietly. "If you are who I hope you are, you can never, *ever* be normal, not ever again." She reached forward and clasped his hand, holding it with a tightness that surprised him. "You are the hero, Howard. You are my Sora's hero."

"I'm not a hero." Hal pulled back. "Anyway, Morgan said there wasn't one, that it was just a trick."

She shook her head almost militantly. "If you want to be a hero, Howard, you will be one."

Hal moved back in his chair, feeling awkward and a little scared. "I didn't do anything. I don't have any powers, Shinju. I'm not even that clever. I wandered in there like an idiot, and nothing happened except that I almost got killed. *He* saved me. And then he sent me away."

Shinju's face fell a little. "You did not break his chains?"

"Well, yes," Hal said. "But Morgan said that was part of your spell."

Shinju folded her arms over her chest, and said nothing.

"I'm not the hero," Hal said again. "Not somebody magic and fated and full of power. But I still want to help him. I don't care why you enchanted me before or who you are or who you think I am. But I want to help him. I want to get back to him. Tell me how."

But Shinju shook her head. "You can't go back," she said. "Not now." When Hal opened his mouth to argue, she shook her head and spoke before he could. "If you aren't the hero, you can't go back."

"Why does that matter?" Hal gestured in the general direction of Santa Monica. "Look, you clearly want someone to help him, and I can see why. I don't like him in there any more than you do. I can tell that you care, so obviously you'd go to him if you could. Just be straight with me this time, and I'll do whatever has to be done."

"It is not that simple." She opened the book and began paging through it while she spoke. "For starters, Morgan can never leave. If he does, he would die, and as soon as he was gone, the Oasis would go with him. You were meant to empower him and to help him retake it. And once this was done, we could once more return."

"We?" Hal asked.

She waved her hand again, and the book turned to another page. It was a drawing, or perhaps more accurately, a painting. It showed a palace of glass and a young boy at its center, tall and thin, dark-haired and fair-faced, his hands outstretched, his eyes staring out from the book into Hal's own. He was content and happy, and love seemed to pour from him into the world around him.

He was Morgan.

"This was long ago," the woman said, her voice full of love and longing, "when he was young." She pointed to the clouds, and

Hal realized there were foxes hidden inside of them—thousands and thousands of foxes—they *were* the clouds.

"Many of us lived inside the sanctuary," Shinju said. "We were his family, and we were all happy. But then Sora matured, and as all children do, he changed. He began to act moody and petulant, and his walls were not as strong as they once had been. And as he sexually matured, he began to ache for his own heart, for someone to love him not as a child but as a man."

She reached up and turned the page. Hal blinked as he saw the same image, though this time there was no love in the boy's eyes, only emptiness. And he looked more like the Morgan he knew, and even more, he looked as Morgan had looked before Hal had fallen asleep: sad, lonely, and empty. In this picture, the glass palace was cracked and shattered, and the clouds behind him were not rosy but dark.

"We did not listen to him," Shinju said, sadly. "*I* did not listen to him. We brought many women before him, but he found them all lacking; finally, one day, he confessed to me that he knew he could take no woman into his heart. I thought, perhaps, since he was born of the sea, he would want some other creature, but he said, no, this was not what he desired. And that was when he told me that he could only love a man. And I did not listen." She shut her eyes. "But Eagan did."

"Eagan was his lover," Hal said grimly.

Shinju nodded. "I made certain to send you when I knew Eagan was away; it was too dangerous otherwise. He is Morgan's false heart. He courted my son in secret, and he wooed him away, convincing him to shut out even his family in pursuit of love, and because Sora was so lonely, he did as Eagan asked. He closed the Oasis to the *kitsune* and took Eagan into his heart. Or, rather, he tried. But Eagan could not go there, because he did not come in love, only in lies, and it changed Sora forever." She smoothed her hand over the page, looking at the boy painted there with sad longing. "Eagan used my son's love to bind him instead, to make him his slave, and so he has remained now for a long, long time. Unless he is freed, he will remain there forever. Only his true love can save him now. His hero."

"Morgan doesn't believe in his true love or in a hero," Hal said.

"It is with the promise of the hero that Eagan binds him," Shinju said grimly. "And therefore the hero must exist in some fashion. Perhaps the potion truly does reveal him. Perhaps he truly can break Morgan's chains. Perhaps not. But what he *does* possess is the magic to free him from his prison—whether he knows it or not." She sighed and leaned back in her chair. "He does, however, have to believe it. In himself. Which I see that you cannot do."

Hal thought again of the sadness in Morgan's eyes and the tenderness he'd felt in his heart. He remembered, too, the way Morgan had denounced his own savior, how certain he was that there was no way out for him, now or ever.

"Why didn't you tell me all this before you sent me in?" he demanded. "Why didn't you tell me how to help him?"

She shook her head. "The hero must make his own way. It was all I could do to give you a bit of protection and glamour and help you see whatever would make it easier for you to fall in love. But it was all for nothing, I see now. Either you cannot be his hero or Eagan has grown too powerful to resist and my son is already lost."

"No," Hal said, his teeth tightening around the word. "He isn't lost. I won't give up on him." When Shinju started to speak, he cut her off. "*Someone* must be able to help him. There has to be

someone who can stop this Eagan—some magician, some warrior—
somebody! If this hero won't show up, then *I* will do it!"

"There are none who can enter but that the heart of the Oasis
lets in," Shinju said. "Only the hero can make his own way."

"*I* got in," Hal reminded her. When she only smiled, faint and
sad, and shook her head, Hal pressed on. "I got in. I drank the
potion. I lived. With Morgan's help, yes, but I did live. I broke his
chains. You said there was something you saw in me that made you
think I could help him. Maybe I'm his hero, maybe I'm not. But
whatever I am, I got in once. I can get in again, if you help me. I just
want to *help him.* Whatever it takes. Whatever it costs."

Shinju looked at him for a long time, her expression
unreadable. When, finally, she spoke, her voice was very quiet.

"I can get you in once more," she said. "And I can enchant you
and give you weapons of great power."

Hal's entire body seemed to sag in relief and then lift just as
quickly in hope. "Then do it."

She held up her hand. "I can get you *in.* But if I do this, I must
overpower the spell that Morgan used to send you away. If I send
you back, Hal Porter, you will have to find your own way out, and
there is a very high likelihood you will not find one at all."

"You mean that I might die?" Hal asked, uneasy but not
unwilling.

She shook her head. "Death would be a blessing compared to
what you will find in their company. The *laumu* will trap you too.
They will find what hell is for you, and they will craft it and use it to
torment you for their own pleasure."

Hal thought of the hell he'd already experienced with the
laumu and of the quiet malice of Eagan and his hulking bodyguards

as they took his job. Then he looked down at the painting of Morgan, shattered and lost.

"What about him?" he asked, quietly. "If I go back and fail, will I make it worse for him?"

Shinju hesitated. "I do not know," she said at last.

For a long time Hal said nothing; he just sat there, his head spinning, flooded with dark memories of the *laumu*, his imagination suggesting tortures and indignities they might devise for him—not just for one night or one month or a year. *Forever.* His chest tightened, too full of fear and self-doubt to allow room for air.

You can't do this, he tried to tell himself. *You'll only make it worse for him and put yourself in hell alongside him.* But then his eyes fell on the image of Morgan—locked in that pain already, *forever*—and Hal's heart ached, shattering the tightness and setting him free.

Yes, hell, a deeper, quiet part of him answered. *But hell with him. With Morgan. Which isn't, really, any kind of hell at all.*

"You must become the hero to go back," Shinju said quietly. Patiently. "You must believe. You must find strength you did not know you had. You must *invent* the strength if you do not have it. And while I can help you find a suitable disguise to enter, and while I can enchant you, once you are inside, you must use your own wits and your own magic. Once you go down this path, Howard Porter, no one can help you but yourself."

Hal nodded, unable to speak for the thickness in his throat. When the pressure became too great, he cleared it and swallowed hard.

"I want to do it," he said, at last. He tightened his fists at his sides and met her eyes. "I *will* do it."

She smiled at him, and he couldn't tell if she was sad or grateful because his vision was suddenly very blurry. He did, though, feel her touch against his face.

"Let us take you back to your home," she said, gently, "and prepare the hero for his battle."

Hal nodded. This time when the world shifted around him and began to fade, it didn't make him queasy at all. Or, at least, no more than he already was.

CHAPTER 6
hal the hunter

THEY reappeared in the hallway outside Hal's apartment, in the dark hollow beneath the stairs where the landlord stored the cleaning equipment he never used. Hal wondered why she hadn't taken him straight into his place, and then he saw the door.

More to the point, he saw the policeman standing in his doorway.

The door was open and the lights were on, and as they stood there in the darkness, Hal heard the man talking to someone just inside, someone standing inside his apartment, but someone he had never met before in his life.

"We meet every Saturday night," the man he couldn't see was saying. He was sniffing a lot, and his voice was high and whiny. "He gives me drugs, and I give him whatever he wants. Which is usually pretty hard-core. Most times I can barely walk home after."

Hal recoiled, and so did the policeman. "Is he a dealer?" the officer asked, holding up a pad of paper as he scribbled furiously on it.

"I don't know," the whiny man said, "but I know where he keeps his stash." He leaned forward, and Hal could finally see his face. It was gaunt and pale and full of blemishes. "You go easier on me, right, the more I tell you? You cut me a deal if I rat him out, right?"

"Sure," the policeman said, absently and without conviction. He peered around the gaunt man—carefully—into the apartment. "You say he has a stash?"

The man laughed. "He has a stash of everything. Drugs, booze, toys, and porn. Likes young ones, apparently. Which makes sense, given how we usually play."

Hal was having trouble breathing. He was hot with embarrassment, cold with terror, and some other indiscernible temperature that registered his rage. What was this shit? Drugs? Prostitution? Pornography? He liked the *young ones?* Hal's hands were opening and closing at his sides. His mouth was open, but before he could so much as squeak, Shinju's hand closed over his wrist.

"That is Eagan," she said very quietly. "This is his spell. He is trying you draw you out." Her hand tightened. "He knows you are near. But he does not know I am with you. I felt him as I brought us here and moved us out of his sight just in time. He will be able to feel you, though."

Eagan. Hal stared at the pock-faced, ugly man leaning out of his apartment and tried to reconcile him with the smooth, handsome man who had been in Gerry's trailer. Actually, outside of the fact that he looked nothing like he'd looked then, the fact that this guy was Eagan made sense. It was the same sort of blindside: swift, unexpected, thorough, and humiliating.

"What am I supposed to do?" he whispered back at Shinju.

"I'll remove us, once he goes back inside. It's too dangerous just now. When he fails to draw you out in anger, he'll try to lure you into a false sense of security and then spring his second trap, which will be worse than this one. But he will also let his guard down enough so that I can take us away without his knowing where we've gone."

Hal felt dizzy, and sick. *Worse than this?* "Why?" he asked. "Why is he doing this?"

"Because you are coming for Morgan," Shinju replied. "Because he fears what you can do."

"*He* fears *me?*" Hal said and then winced as the tart in his doorway displayed an array of bites and hickeys across his abdomen, which, allegedly, Hal had given him.

"Yes," Shinju said, "but he's counting on your continuing to sell yourself short, which you're doing an excellent job of right now, I might add." She turned him away from Eagan and held his face in her hands so he had to look her in the eye. "You have more power than he does. Always remember that, Howard. *Always.*"

"I think I know his computer passwords," Eagan said, still whining. He wiped an anorexic arm beneath his nose and gestured inside. "He told me about some kinky thing he had going at one of the parks. Maybe that will help you stop some poor innocent kid from turning up like me, huh?" He snorted a laugh and led the policeman inside.

It was all so bizarre, so over the top—Hal wanted to leap out and shake the officer and ask him if he really believed all that shit, just like that, from some junkie? God in heaven, it was *killing him* to stand here and listen to this! But he held still, bit his tongue and, when nothing else would work, shut his eyes and ran through an imaginary rosary. Certainly, if God had to choose between him and Eagan, he could count on the upper hand here at least.

After a few minutes of silence, Shinju took his hand again. "I will take us a little way from here, and we can regroup." Hal nodded, keeping his eyes shut. He felt himself begin to fade, and he let go a sigh of relief. But as they went back into the mist, he felt an invisible slap across his mind and then heard Eagan's wicked laugh before he whispered a parting shot at him. It faded as quickly as it came, but when he felt himself become solid again, he turned to Shinju, heartsick and full of panic.

"Mother," he choked, trying not to throw up. "He said he's going to go after my *mother.*"

Shinju's eyebrows shot up into her hairline. "He truly is frightened, then, if he's making that kind of threat." When Hal began to sputter, she patted his arm gently. "It's empty. He can't touch her."

"He can call her on the phone," Hal shot back. He pulled away from Shinju and began to pace like a caged animal. They were in a narrow alley, and he all but bounced between the two brick walls. "Even the tamest of that bile he was spouting would hurt her more than if he put a knife into her chest."

"Your mother would judge you so easily, by the words of a stranger?" Shinju said, unconvinced.

"I don't want her to even *hear* that!" Hal shouted.

Shinju held up a hand. "I will protect her," she said, trying to calm him. "I doubt he would reach that far, even if he could, but I will protect her just in case. Does that ease you?"

"A little." Hal stopped pacing, but he shoved his hands into his hair. "How am I supposed to fight him? How can I possibly have more power than he does?"

"You have a different sort of power." Shinju raised an eyebrow. "Do you still mean to go? Or has he succeeded, and you are now convinced you cannot defeat him?"

"I don't think for a minute that I can defeat him," Hal said, "but I'm still going to go." He lowered his hands, trying to regain his composure. "You can really keep him from my mother?"

"I can, and I will," Shinju assured him. "You should call her, before you go."

Hal looked down at himself and then put his hand over the bulge of his cell phone in his jeans pocket. "I don't even know what to tell her," he said.

"You tell her what she wants to hear," Shinju said. "That you love her and that you will call her again soon."

"She wants to hear that I've gotten married," Hal said, sighing as he pulled out his phone. His heart sank as he saw that it was out of battery.

"You can tell her that after you rescue Morgan," she said.

"They made that illegal again in California," Hal said and raised his cell phone. "Also, my phone is dead."

"Morgan is not in California. He is his own land and his own law. Or he will be, once he is free from Eagan." She nodded at his phone. "Try it again."

Hal looked at the phone, and he wasn't even surprised as he watched the battery meter go from empty to fully charged.

"I'll wait at the opening of the alley," she said, starting down into the mist as she spoke. "Take whatever time you need."

Hero

Hal nodded his thanks, opened his phone, and dialed. It was ringing as he lifted it to his ear, and she answered on the second ring.

"Hi, Mom." He smiled. "No, nothing's wrong. I just felt like calling, that's all." He looked out into the darkness, and his heart constricted. "Do you have time to talk?"

She did, of course, and so they talked, and Hal did not rush her in any way. In fact, he encouraged every side story, every odd bit of news, even the repeats from last week or the month before. When she ran out of things to tell him, he asked her questions, one after another, until he, too, had run dry. Even then he lingered, unwilling to let it end.

"I hope you're planning to go to church on Sunday," she said, to fill the silence.

Hal had not been to church in four years. "Do you remember when I wanted to build a church?" he said instead. "Remember the drawing I showed Father Timothy?"

"Your cathedral!" she said, and laughed fondly. "Oh, my, but it was the church of all churches, wasn't it? All glass and towers. It looked like a piece of crystal floating in the sky."

Hal had forgotten that. He only remembered the way Father Timothy had dismissed him. He had forgotten the drawing itself. He tried to see the image in his mind, but he couldn't. He could only see Morgan.

"A palace of glass," his mother said, still wistful. "I believe I said something foolish, that I wouldn't want to have to clean it. But it was very beautiful, Hal. I should have told you that." She paused and then said reluctantly, "I should have told you that more often."

"That my drawing was beautiful?" Hal teased her but gently, because his heart was feeling warm.

"That you were beautiful," his mother said firmly. "That what you did was beautiful. You have so much talent—you always did. But I was afraid it would go to your head, so I tried to ground you." She sighed. "Sometimes I think I grounded you too much."

Hal felt his face warm, and for a moment he didn't know what to say. Then he remembered what lay ahead of him, and his awkwardness fled. "You did just fine, Mom," he said, not gruffly anymore. "You did just fine."

"I wish you would come home more often," she said sadly.

"I might not be home for awhile." Hal reached out and stroked the brick of the wall before him.

"Hal," she said her voice very faint now, and Hal knew she was trying not to let him hear her cry. "Something's wrong, and I can hear it in your voice, so don't try to tell me it isn't. You're upset about something that you have to tell me."

Hal felt miserable. "Mom—"

"No," she said, her voice suddenly firm, interrupting him. "You just listen. Before you tell me this, I only want to know one thing. Whatever this is, is it good? Will this make you happy, Howard?"

Hal paused. Happy? He thought of the hell waiting for him back at the Oasis, and he started to say no. Then he saw Morgan's face, and he remembered the way being with him had made him feel. "Maybe," he said.

"Good," she said, a little stronger. "Then whatever it is, it's fine."

Hal realized, his face flushing, that his mother had gotten the wrong idea about why he was calling. "Mom," he said, hesitantly.

"I *know*, Howard," she said quietly. "I've known a long time."

"Know?" he repeated, confused. "Know what?"

"That you're gay, Hal."

Hal pulled the phone back briefly and looked at it in surprise. Odd, he thought. He should feel panic. Fear. Somehow, he didn't. He only felt... surprise.

He put it back to his ear, but it took him a few moments to speak. "You—knew? *That*?"

"I'm your *mother*, Howard."

He thought of the *Catholic Digest* wedding article flanked by twenties. "But you were always telling me about the girls you wanted me to date back home!"

"Well, I'd tell you about the boys, but I don't know which of them would be interested, because I'm not *their* mother, and I thought it might be nice if *you* told *me* first that that was the sort of partner you were after," she said a bit testily.

Hal's head was swimming. All this time. All this time, he'd been so full of shame, always hiding, and *all this time*, his own *mother* had been waiting for him to come out?

He leaned back against the wall of the building, suddenly requiring it to hold him upright.

"The point of the matter is, Howard," she went on, "that I raised you to have a good head and a generous heart. I raised you *very well*. There are people who say I should have remarried after your father died, that I should have tried to toughen you up, but I never saw it that way. I armed you with love. I don't see that I can do any better than that." Her voiced gentled. "And I'll love whoever it is that you love, sweetheart."

For a few minutes, Hal felt like it was hard to breathe, like his heart was swollen inside his chest. He realized after several seconds that he was smiling, too, a huge, ridiculous smile that made his cheeks hurt. He laughed. "Well, I *have* to be a good man. I've been through every single edition of *Catholic Digest* since 1998. Cover to cover."

"I love you, Howard," she said, her voice less firm than it had been a moment ago but not sad. Then she added, "Is he a nice boy?"

"He's wonderful," Hal said without hesitation. Or, he realized, his smile widening, guilt. "He's a little zany. But he has a big heart. You'd love him, Mom." Hal drew a breath and then shut his eyes. "I love *you*, Mom."

"I love you too," his mother said, and he could hear her smile. "Take care of yourself. And give my love to your nice young man."

"I will," Hal whispered back. Then he cleared his throat, straightened his shoulders and said, with more self-assurance, "I will." He gripped the phone tightly in his hand. "Good-bye, Mom."

"Good-bye, my son," she replied. And then she was gone.

Hal composed himself and came out of the alley. He wasn't surprised to find Shinju waiting for him.

"I'm ready," he said.

She nodded and extended her hand toward him. Hal glanced around the street and looked further out toward the mountains, imagining the land that rolled out all the way to Kansas. He whispered good-bye once more. Then he reached out and put his hand in Shinju's and let her lead him away.

Hero

ONCE again, Hal and Shinju traversed many miles across the city as easily as if they were crossing the street. It would be a handy skill anywhere, but Hal was pretty sure its highest value would be measured here in Los Angeles. The irony was, of all the times he would have appreciated a nice traffic snarl to sort through his thoughts, this time would have been at the top of his list. As it was, they arrived back at the construction site far too soon. The lot, he saw, was empty again. God help him, was he supposed to make that happen too?

Shinju noticed his agitation and smiled at him as she took both his hands, pressing them together between her own. He felt something forming slowly inside them; when she let him go, he opened his palms and startled when he saw. It was the large pearl from the center of her necklace. He looked up to confirm and saw that it was indeed gone from her strand, lodged now inside the palm of his hand.

"It will help protect you," she said.

Hal brushed his thumb against the fat pearl in his hand. It was warm and heavy. It felt like a lot more than a pearl. As he turned it between his fingers, he felt strange memories stir inside his mind, memories that weren't his own. This was *big* magic.

"Put it in your mouth and swallow it," she told him.

Hal felt a little creepy, still not sure exactly what this thing was, but he did as she said. It filled his mouth, but as soon as it hit his tongue, it began to shrink, and so he swallowed quickly. It tasted like honey and cinnamon. As it slid down his throat, he felt strange and thick, as if his insides were rewriting themselves. It wasn't that much different than the potion. It elicited the same queasiness inside him.

"The *laumu* are clannish, young, and spiteful," Shinju said. "They fear what is different. They don't like outsiders." She removed the pearl earring from her right ear and brought it up to Hal's left. "Which is why we will make certain they cannot perceive you as one this time. I will send you in as a Hunter, one of their oafish 'pets' that patrol the borders of the Oasis to trap *kitsune* and unlucky humans. You will appear in your true form outside, but once you cross the border, you will appear as one of them and they will not be able to tell who you truly are, no matter what magic they use. So long as you wear my earring, the spell will be impenetrable."

"What's the pearl I swallowed for?" Hal asked, watching the earring gleam softly in her hand.

"Something else," she said and nodded at his ear. "Hold still, and I will put the earring in place."

"Wait," Hal said, "I don't have—"

He cried out as she stuck the earring through the virgin flesh of his ear, but he didn't fight her. He just stood there, gritting his teeth and feeling the blood drip onto his shoulder as she secured the earring in place. When she was finished, she came and stood in front of him, looking pleased.

"You are a good and loyal warrior," she said.

"I'm a construction worker," Hal reminded her. "That's all."

"Yes," she agreed, still pleased. "You build things. That is always good." She gestured to the empty lot. "You may go inside now. They will not stop you. They will not recognize you so long as you wear my earring. And my soul will protect you. Go now, hero. Go to Morgan."

"That's it?" Hal glanced around, panicking. "I swallow part of your necklace and wear your earring, and that will do it?"

Hero

"You have with you now all the magic and protection I can give you," Shinju said, "but they are nothing compared to what you carry in your heart."

"But I don't know what to *do*!" Hal cried. "You keep telling me that I have power and magic, but I don't feel it. I just feel like myself. The same self I've ever been. How is that going to save him?" He gestured behind him, at the place where the bar should be. "It isn't even here, Shinju! I can't go inside because it isn't even here!"

"You are human, Howard Porter," she said, as if he was silly to have forgotten. "You are more magical and powerful than any other creature in the universe. Do you honestly think you should be able to walk around conscious of that too?"

"If I'm supposed to use it," he shot back, "then, yes!"

But he felt softened somehow, all the same. The most magical creature in the universe? Him? Well, as a human, yes, but—really? *Him?*

Shinju smiled and gestured to indicate the length of him. "Your disguise will appear as soon as you step inside, and to help you, I will send along a little bit of myself as well to aid your disguise. Trust yourself, Howard Porter. Trust yourself, your instincts, and your heart, and you will have whatever victory you desire." She took a step backward, melting away as Hal watched her. "I will wait here to congratulate you on your success." Then the woman was gone. Hal saw, in the distance, a white fox with nine tails trotting off into the night, though he also noticed it was limping a little too.

Hal stared at the place where she had gone, his ear still pounding, his insides still unsettled, and his doubt churning like a sea. He stepped off the sidewalk onto the empty lot, and he saw the building appear, the same as it had been the night before. In the distance he saw dark shapes skulking again. *Hunters,* he realized. These were the Hunters. Looking for him.

And he was about to become one of them temporarily.

Hal tugged at his dingy T-shirt and jeans, smoothed his hand over his sweat-damp hair, and looked up at the door swelling ahead of him in darkness, wafting stale, putrid air out at his face. He reached into his jeans, found his St. Thomas medal-turned-fox-coin, squeezed it tightly, and then went inside.

NOTHING about the interior of the bar was the same as it had been the night before.

Hal supposed he should have expected it, but it jarred him all the same. The walls weren't even in the same places. The ceiling was higher. Last night it had been a smoky pub; tonight it was a giant dance club, complete with flashing lights and cagelike stages where, inside what looked like showers of glitter, dancers bent their bodies in time to pounding, pulsing music. The floor was filled with dancers, too, decked out in outrageous costumes again, but they were different this time. He recognized none of the faces, not even any of the hair. Tonight they were, in fact, mostly bald. There were also large men in black stationed all around the room, surveying the crowd with stern, suspicious glances, their faces glowing red as furnaces.

And in the center of it all, he saw Morgan.

He wasn't sure how he knew the lithe, shockingly redheaded dancer in the center was Morgan—he looked nothing like he had the night before in any of his incarnations. And to add to the confusion, he once again appeared to be female. Hal worried that he was enchanted again, but then he saw passers-by teasing Morgan, pointing at his breasts and trying to pinch him. One pulled up his skirt, too, and Hal blinked as he saw that the transformation, apparently, had been complete. For whatever reason, someone had compelled Morgan to play a girl.

But even though this time the change was more than just an illusion, somehow Hal had no problem seeing through it. It was as if, despite the lie of his eyes, his heart could see the truth. His eyes saw breasts that were slight but obviously present—the twin mounds bounced in time to Morgan's movements beneath a black leather halter—and curves and a narrower jaw and shoulders, but his heart saw the true Morgan, the one who had made love to him.

Morgan was once again decked out with chains, except this time the chains were much thicker and looked heavier. The collar at his neck was thick and bulky, and it hooked to the fattest chain of all, which dangled over his shoulder, attaching itself to the top of the cage. The cage itself hung suspended over the dance floor, though right now it was low to the ground, giving the dancers on the floor beside him a chance to taunt him or to reach in and pinch him, torments that many of them were indulging in regularly. Morgan looked as if he were trying to ignore them, but there was no hiding his blushes or the misery that played across his face. Hal knew it had everything to do with Hal's own visit to and escape from the bar, and he ached. He stepped forward, upset and wanting to put an end to this, and stopped short as he caught sight of himself in a mirrored pillar.

Morgan was very changed, yes. But his alteration was nothing to Hal's.

If the reflection hadn't been moving in exact concert to Hal's movements, he would never have suspected the man he saw staring back was him. He looked taller and thinner. His face was narrower and his eyes smaller, but his nose was bigger, he had two curving horns like a ram, and his chin—Jesus, was that supposed to be a goatee? He looked like some sort of devil. And the outfit didn't help. He wore black leather pants that, on closer reflection, he realized were chaps, swallowed from the knee on down by stiff leather boots with—God help him—heels. Not stilettos, at least, but they were definitely platforms. They didn't make any damn sense—how did anybody hunt in *these*? He had on some sort of red underwear, too, except the noticeable draft against his backside told him that his dick was the only thing covered. He didn't even feel the ridge of a thong. His ass was just bare, plain and simple. As bare as his chest, which was actually rather close to his own, though bulkier and hairier. A lot hairier.

This was a *laumu* Hunter? This oversexed freak show in high heels—*this?* What did they do, fuck their prey to death?

Hal stared at himself, feeling very self-conscious and a little angry. But as he gawked, his reflection shook its head and held a finger to its lips. It pointed down to a white bag attached to his waist and patted it. Then it gestured to the dance floor.

Hal followed his reflection's gesture, trying not to look as frightened and uncertain as he felt. He felt the eyes of the room swing toward him, and some instinct told him he shouldn't stay on the dais but should go down the stairs. It was odd how easily he could move on those heels, and he stopped feeling so ridiculous as he realized that he was the only one in the room who thought that he was. In fact, everyone else seemed to be a little bit afraid of him. They kept looking at his waist, at his bag, whispering and pointing, their eyes going wide. Hal didn't let himself look down, but he felt carefully against the bag. It was furry, and soft, and he felt something attached to it, something like… a foot. An animal's foot. He had to look down. There was a tail, as well: a full tail, thick and bushy, and as white as the foot.

I will send a bit of myself along with you, she'd said. And then he remembered the limp.

Hal dropped the foot, trying not to gag.

Several black-clad men were converging on him, but cautiously; they were flanking a tall man with long, shining white hair, dressed in what Hal was pretty sure was silk: blue silk shirt and silvery silk pants lined with runes. His feet were bare, revealing—to Hal's dismay—a pair of hooves. The white-haired man, unlike his escorts, was not cautious, only curious. And it was in that lazy, unconcerned stare that Hal recognized him. This was Eagan.

He had a cigarette in his hand, and he reached out and tapped the ash from the end idly onto the floor.

"Well, Hunter," he said at last and gestured to Hal's waist. "You have a prize for me, I see."

A *laumu* man appeared beside Hal almost out of nowhere; the man was bald and taller than the rest, and he had a very odd and crooked nose, but when his eyes met Hal's there was no mistaking that it was Talin who was hovering there. Hal glared, and to his surprise, Talin paled and then bowed low.

"Sir," he said, breathless and clearly frightened. "Sir, if you please?" He gestured to the paw and the tail, and Hal realized that he meant for Hal to hand them over.

Hal hesitated. These weren't just *from* Shinju. They were, quite literally, part of her. Should he really just hand them over, just like that?

Eagan rolled his eyes. "You'll be compensated," he said wearily. He drew on his cigarette again. "I know we had a bit of fun with the last Hunter who came here, but we're bored with that sort of thing now. Just give us the goods, and we'll get you your bounty."

Hal hoped the Hunter disguise also hid his panic. In the end, he reached down and undid the ties that held the tail and foot in place, trying not to let his hands shake. Likely Shinju wouldn't care. Anyone willing to cut their feet and tail off were likely willing to go all the way. He handed them both to Talin, unable to resist curling his lip at him as he did so. To his delight, Talin cringed and darted away more quickly than necessary.

Eagan passed his cigarette to one of his bodyguards without looking to see if they were ready to take it and accepted the tail and foot from Talin. His expression remained neutral, but his gray eyes danced with malice. "Ah, yes, it's genuine *kitsune*. An *old* one, by the look of it." He held up the tail and paused. His eyes narrowed as he leaned forward and smelled the fur. Then he drew back, eyes wide and gleaming. "Surely it *can't be*—!" He turned to Hal. "When did you get this? *Where?*"

"In an alley," Hal said, hoping that was somewhere a Hunter might attack a *kitsune*. "Not far from here."

Eagan's grin was terrible. "Was a human with her? A human male?"

Hal faltered. Should he lie and let Eagan think he was dead? Would Eagan want a body? "No," he said and held his breath.

Eagan seemed disappointed. "It wasn't her, then. I felt the bitch with him at the human's apartment as they tried to leave. Ah, well. That's the next bounty for you, though," he said, winking at Hal. "If you catch *them,* I'll let you go on whatever rampage you like."

"It isn't the *kitsune* queen?" Talin asked, peering at Shinju's tail and paw.

Eagan shook his head. "I can't be certain. And at any rate, it's the human who is the real danger now." He smiled slowly, turning toward the dance floor with a very wicked expression. "But we can still have some fun with these. It doesn't matter who they actually belong to, does it? It matters to whom our Morgan *believes* they do."

Hal was forgotten now; everyone around him followed Eagan as he sauntered up to Morgan's cage. He dispersed the tormentors and leaned up against the gilded bars.

"Darling," he said brightly, "a Hunter's just come in, and he brought the most extraordinary thing. I thought you might like to see it."

God, he was *cruel*, Hal thought, tensing as he watched Morgan frown at the tail and paw and then recoil, blood draining from his face he stared at them.

"That's one of the old ones," Morgan said, his voice pinched high to match his body. He looked sick. "Who was it?"

Eagan grinned. "Come now. It hasn't been *that* long. Surely you recognize *her.*"

Morgan's face was now white. "No," he whispered, tears forming in his eyes. "No! No! *No!*" He sobbed, once, and then clamped his hands over his mouth and sank to the floor. "*Mama!*"

It took every ounce of Hal's control to keep from both rushing forward to comfort Morgan and body slamming Eagan into the floor before he beat that leering grin right off his face. *Why?* he wanted to scream at him. *Why are you so needlessly cruel?* He enjoyed it, Morgan had said, and Hal hadn't believed it could be that simple, but as he stood here, watching the man laugh as Morgan sobbed over what he believed to be all that remained of his mother, Hal realized that, actually, it really was that crude. Eagan was apparently what you got when you surgically removed someone's sense of empathy, but he was worse because he didn't just not feel anyone else's pain; he fed off the interesting spectacle it made. He got a high off of other people's misery, the more exquisite the better. In short, he made regular sociopaths look downright friendly.

Now he was done with Morgan, and he was turning back toward Hal.

"Well!" he said breezily, wiping tears of laughter from his eyes. "That was well worth your bounty!" He took one last breath to collect himself and smiled at Hal. "As a thank you, I'll grant you not only the usual license of two humans to do with what you see fit— just remember, you must catch them between sunrise and sunset— but I'll toss in a bit of tail too." He laughed at his own joke and gestured to the room. "Anyone you like, to fuck however you like, until sunrise. Except me, of course."

Several *laumu* cried out in alarm, and Hal caught several of their shapes flickering out of the corners of his eye. Eagan saw it, too, and laughed again.

"Oh my," he said. "It seems suddenly my court is made up of nothing but fat old men. Dear me. Your pickings are slim, Hunter, I'm afraid." Then his eyes fell on Morgan's cage—and gleamed. "Ah—yes, of course! I forgot. We have one *very special* lady left for you."

Hal was very glad for his disguise in that moment, because he knew that if he hadn't had a face full of horns and warts and too-sharp teeth, his shock and confusion would have been written there plainly instead. And the benefit of having blood-red skin was, he realized, that no one had any idea when he blushed. He wanted to be angry with Eagan again, but he was too busy being wary as he watched the *laumu* man amble back toward Morgan's cage again. Was it actually going to be this simple? Or was this another trick? It had to be—there was no way Eagan was going to *give* Morgan to him.

Hero

But no, actually, that's exactly what he was doing, Hal realized, watching as Eagan unlocked the door to Morgan's cage, unhooked the chains, and then began to drag him out of it. Morgan fought him, still sobbing, but when he realized where Eagan was taking him, he began to shout and kick as well.

"You *bastard!*" he screamed, in his woman's voice. "You *can't!* You can't make me service the monster that killed my mother! You *can't!*"

"Not only *can* I," Eagan purred back, "but I'm going to watch it happen. Right here in the middle of the dance floor, *lover.*"

Morgan swore at him, and Hal shut his eyes for a moment, murmuring Hail Marys under his breath. *In the middle of the dance floor.* Eagan was going to make Hal rape Morgan, right here in front of everyone. Morgan's swearing had turned to sobs again, and Eagan was glaring at him in disgust as he shouted for someone to bring him a Stiff Drink. Hal watched Morgan curl into a tight, despairing ball and something snapped inside him.

That was it. That was *it.* He wasn't letting them hurt Morgan, not anymore. He took a step forward, fists clenched at his sides, ready to take Eagan apart with his bare hands. He didn't care if it was a stupid idea. He just couldn't stand here and watch this horseshit any longer.

But as he took a second step, he felt something slide against his leg and *clink* softly on the floor. He stopped, looked down, and saw his St. Thomas medal lying there, glinting in the lights.

Hal paused, and then he bent down and picked up the transformed medal. He stared at it for a moment before sliding it back into his pocket. It didn't occur to him until after he'd done it that his Hunter outfit didn't *have* pockets—he'd put it into his jeans. Which, apparently, he was still wearing somehow, despite appearances otherwise.

He looked down at Morgan, who was gagging as two *laumu* forced him to down another sizzling glass of elixir. Hal watched Morgan's eyes go dull, but it didn't upset him now. Not anymore.

Hold on, Morgan, he whispered quietly, and reached down to touch his St. Thomas medal through his jeans. *I'll find my magic somehow, and I will save you. I'm not a hero. But I'll make myself one for you.*

He pulled his hand away from the medal and stepped forward and met Eagan grin for leering grin.

CHAPTER 7
Morgan Dances

HE HAD to find a way to let Morgan know he was Hal, not a Hunter. Thinking about having to sexually assault him for the *laumu*'s enjoyment, whether or not Morgan knew who was doing it, was something his brain could not quite process, so he focused on the details it could. He didn't know how he was going to defeat Eagan, but he knew he would have a lot better shot if he had an ally. And the only one he had here was Morgan.

Morgan, who was swaying on the floor where he sat, trying to fight the elixir as it took over his system and the others laughed. Morgan, who was looking at Hal with so much wounded hate it nearly brought him to his knees.

And the Oasis's emotional upset, Hal realized, was starting to show in the very structure of the bar. The walls were wiggling like Jell-O, and the lights and disco balls were swaying. When the floor buckled, Hal stopped short and looked around in panic. But the others only laughed.

"It does that when he's upset," Eagan said without concern. His grin darkened. "Pardon me—I misspoke, didn't I? When *she* is upset." He nodded at Morgan. "Go on. Have her. We're eager to see what you do."

The others were giggling now—several had shifted back into more pleasing shapes, though some apparently were taking no chances and remained ugly. And male, Hal noticed. Even the pretty ones still had a masculine look about them. All of them, though, were giggling like twelve-year-olds. Hal thought about his sexually charged costume for a moment and then thought about what Gerry had said to him about the assaults in the empty lot. And what Eagan had promised him: two humans. Something told Hal they would be females.

Hal looked back at Morgan, feeling sicker than before. He had to find a way to let him know. He *had* to.

Eagan clapped his hands and made a hurry-up gesture. "Perhaps you would like to begin with a lap dance, sir? She is particularly good at that, I must confess." He winked and favored Hal with a wicked smile. The other dancers had all stopped by this point, and as Eagan spoke, someone brought a chair out into the middle of the floor.

Hal walked over to it as smoothly as he could. The heels really were high. But he noticed that when he started to lose his balance, it was as if something invisible caught him and righted him. He passed another mirrored pillar, and he was surprised to find that, though he felt nervous and uncertain and a bit sick, his face looked mean and even eager. Even when he gasped in surprise and blinked, his expression as reflected in the mirror remained the grisly expression of a Hunter.

Shinju's disguise, apparently, was very thorough. He reached up and touched the earring in his still swollen ear. Of course, that was only going to make the job of showing Morgan who he truly was even more difficult.

He looked worriedly at Morgan as he sat down in the chair. Several *laumu* were hoisting Morgan up and aiming him at Hal, but Morgan looked almost catatonic now. And pained—oh, God, but he looked so shattered. When they pushed him forward, propelling him at Hal, he came in a tumble of legs and arms. As Morgan fell into Hal's lap, one last sob escaped him, and then he simply went limp and quiet.

The *laumu* were jeering and shouting and laughing, and Hal's heart was breaking. How? He didn't even think Morgan would hear him anymore. Even if he could, what words to say? "Morgan, it's me, Hal?" The *laumu* were so close. They might hear. It would take many loud words to penetrate Morgan's pain and make him understand. It would be too much risk. If he could get him to look at him, maybe he could try that telepathy thing—but Morgan wouldn't, not anymore. Hal tightened his fists and began to sweat. Oh, he wished he *did* have that magic that Shinju was so sure he had.

And then he remembered, and he laughed out loud. It came out sounding like a grunt, and the *laumu* only giggled, but he didn't care. Grinning, Hal reached into his jeans pocket and pulled out the coin. He kept it hidden inside the Hunter's huge right hand and made a show of stroking Morgan's red hair with his left. Morgan flinched and the *laumu* cheered, and while they were all distracted, Hal pressed the melted medal as subtly as he could into Morgan's palm.

Too late, he realized his mistake—Morgan startled and turned to him, his dull eyes sharp again with new pain and then blurry as tears ran down his face. *He thinks a Hunter has killed me.* Hal started to shake his head but stopped, worried that Shinju's spell would hide that too. He tried to shout into Morgan's mind, but it didn't work, either because of his disguise or because he was so nervous. He tried to think of something they had talked about, something they had done that would let Morgan know it was him—*I could describe his room to him,* Hal thought. But Morgan was starting to turn away, trying to push away, and Hal panicked.

"I love you," he said. And to his surprise, the words came out in his own voice.

Morgan stopped. Then he turned and looked at Hal.

Hal didn't look away from him, but he braced, watching out of the corner of his eye to see if the *laumu* had heard him. But they were still laughing and jeering and urging him to *fuck her hard!* They hadn't heard him.

But Morgan had.

His eyes were sharp now, focus coming through the haze of the drug, and though tears still clung to his eyelashes, they weren't falling any longer. He stared at Hal so hard that Hal could feel the gaze burning the back of his skull. Hal tried again to speak through his mind—*Morgan, it's me, it's Hal! Howard! It's me, Howard! I've come to save you, but I don't know how, and I can't rape you, but they're going to make me, and I'm sorry that this is the worst rescue ever, but it's me, Morgan—your mother's alive, and it's me!* But he could feel the words bouncing back, not arriving. He couldn't reach him. He just had to hope and pray.

Morgan looked strange, as if he were trying hard not to hope. He looked down at his hand, where the coin was hidden. Then he looked back at Hal.

"What was this?" he asked, very quietly. "This coin you gave me. What was it before it was a coin?"

Hal couldn't help it. He grinned. "A medal," he whispered. It was the Hunter's voice again, but he didn't care. "A St. Thomas medal that my mother gave me. Your mother changed it." He reached out to touch Morgan's face again. "Your mother is alive, Morgan. Your mother is alive, and so am I."

The *laumu* had started to quiet, their laughs turned to murmurs and whispers. Eagan had retreated to a table nearby to watch, and Hal could see him lifting his head from conversation, trying to figure out what was wrong.

"They're onto me, I think," Hal said, worried. "It's probably the way you're looking at me, like you'd like to throw your arms around me and kiss me."

Morgan was weeping again, but he was smiling too. "I can't help it." He touched Hal's face in wonder. "Why did you come back?"

Hal couldn't help it either. He put his big, fat hands on Morgan's tiny waist—but if he really looked, he could see his real hands and Morgan's real body too. *Just illusion,* he thought. *Our bodies are just illusions. It's the people beneath we love.* He smiled as he looked up at Morgan's face. "I already told you why I came back."

Morgan went a little slack in his arms, bent forward, and pressed a kiss to his mouth. "I love you too," he whispered.

"What the devil is this?" Eagan demanded, and stalked angrily toward them.

I think we're screwed, Hal started to say and then gagged as something filled his throat. He pulled back, alarmed, and then coughed as whatever it was that choked him pushed against his windpipe and then shot out of his mouth. Morgan caught it, and when Hal had recovered, he saw Morgan staring down at Shinju's pearl in his hand. He laughed.

"Oh Mama." His voice was breathless. "Thank you." Then he looked up at Hal with a wicked gleam in his eye. "Follow my lead," he said and then rose and turned around.

Eagan stopped, but he was looking at Morgan warily. Morgan bent forward a little, letting his cleavage flash as he made a strange little purr.

"Now, *don't,*" he said, and made a wide, drunken *go-away* gesture at Eagan. "You *told* me to dance for him, and I'm *going* to dance for him, but this music is *awful.*" He put his hands on his hips, swaying a bit as he pouted. "*Change* it."

Eagan was looking at Morgan with narrowed eyes. "All done sobbing, then?" he asked, his voice full of suspicion.

Morgan blinked and then looked around in confusion. "What?"

Hal decided it was time for him to play backup. Apparently Morgan *wanted* to dance. He glanced at Morgan's two clenched fists, one with the pearl, one with the coin. He grunted and shifted on his chair. "I thought I was supposed to get fucked," he said. The words tasted bad in his mouth, and he hadn't been sure he'd put the right emphasis on them, but once again Shinju's spell came through: they came out gruff and growly, and the sound of them almost startled him.

Morgan picked up his cue, swayed again, and giggled. "I feel so funny." Then he cooed and ran his hands down his body, still clutching the two objects. "Ooh, I feel so *funny.*"

Eagan was still watching Morgan carefully, but now he was smiling again. "Ah. I think, perhaps, we gave you a bit too much elixir, darling."

Morgan stumbled forward and fell against him. "Will you fuck me?" he asked, in his soft, sultry female voice.

Eagan reached down and pinched Morgan's bottom and then slapped it. "You have to dance first, my love. And you have to fuck a Hunter. In front of us. Is that a problem?"

Morgan was clinging to Eagan now, squirming against his hand as it slid beneath her skirt. "Eagan, I'm so *hot*," he whined. The pearl and coin were gone now, but Hal was sure somehow that Morgan still had them.

Eagan laughed and shoved Morgan back toward Hal. "Dance, my little slut. Work for your fuck." He snapped his fingers and nodded at one of the bodyguards who had come up beside him. "See to the music."

And then Morgan was stumbling forward, straddling Hal's legs. The music began, and Morgan smiled wickedly as he reached up to slide the straps of his skimpy top off his shoulders.

"I'm going to get us out of here," he said quietly, still stripping slowly as he ground his hips against Hal's legs. "But I want to take a little revenge first, if you don't mind."

"Sure," Hal said, and he jolted when Morgan's top fell away and his breasts fell out. He felt himself bracing as Morgan brought them closer and then chastised himself. It was still Morgan. He'd been attracted to him before as a woman. Why not now? But he couldn't stop staring at the breasts. They were just so *big*. And *round*. The female Morgan before, at least, had been pretty damn butch.

As if Morgan could read his mind, he smiled and shook his head. "Don't worry, lover," he said, his woman's voice sultry. Then it dropped into the octave Hal remembered as Morgan said, "I remember what you like."

Hal sucked in a breath as Morgan's body shimmered, and suddenly, the man he'd made love to was before him again.

"Only you can see me like this. The rest of them see me in the form that Eagan forced on me." Morgan reached up and stroked his face. His long black hair was floating around him, his lean, male chest brushing against Hal's as he leaned forward to nuzzle kisses along his jaw. "Touch me, Howard," he whispered. "Touch me, and I'll dance for you."

Hal could smell him. He smelled like Morgan, like a man, and when he ran his hand up Morgan's side, fumbling carefully for a breast, his hand traveled up a flat, smooth plane until he hit Morgan's small, pebbled nipple. Unable to stop himself, he tweaked it and shuddered as Morgan purred into his ear. The *laumu* clapped and began to hoot, but Morgan brushed a kiss against his cheek and then whispered again.

"Make love to me, Howard," he said. "Make love to me now, while they watch, not knowing who you are or how much I love you."

The music was pulsing now, loud and strange and hypnotic all around him, and Morgan was sliding his hands against Hal's body, grinding his hips against the thin fabric of the Hunter's thong. Morgan reached down and lifted the skirt, and when he pressed against Hal again, he could feel his lover's erection rubbing against his own.

Hal hesitated. He was aroused, yes, but he was self-conscious, too, and uneasy. *I'm not like this,* he protested, but quietly and only to himself. *This isn't me.* But then, out of nowhere, the memory of that male dancer at the bachelorette party wafted before him—the dancer who, quite accidentally, had sealed the argument on Hal's uncertain sexuality. And he realized, as the ten-year-old memory surfaced again, that it wasn't just that he'd wanted the man. He'd wanted to be the one the man was grinding against in the chair, in front of everyone.

Hal looked up at Morgan, and it felt like he was looking up through a thirty-years-tall cage of *Catholic Digests,* a tower of fear and shame and uncertainty. But Morgan only smiled and ground against him again and kissed him.

And the tower shuddered and fell as Hal opened his mouth, taking his lover inside as the *laumu* cheered him on.

IT WAS surprisingly easy, Hal found, to make out with someone in front of a crowd. The part of his brain that sounded suspiciously like the nun he'd had for a teacher in sixth grade, finding itself unable to get anywhere whatsoever with guilt and shame, spent its time speculating as to why, exactly, this was true. Oddly, part of it seemed to be because Hal's little performance was being done in front of strangers, and even better, it was in front of strangers who already hated him and were openly mocking him—both his true self and his disguise. It was strangely freeing. The worst, in a sense, had already happened. The fear that lurked in the back of his mind was always that he might be exposed as a sinner and go down in other people's esteem. But these people would hate him no matter what. There wasn't any way for shame to get traction here.

It also helped that Morgan was absolutely, no question about it, the sexiest thing Hal had ever seen. He hadn't been joking when he'd said he knew what Hal liked; he'd taken his "base form," as he'd called it, the one that Hal had found so beautiful, and right now that form was grinding and sliding against his body in time to some incredibly slutty music. Hal couldn't make out the words, but he didn't need them because Morgan was urging him on with his own.

"Touch me," he begged as he stroked Hal's head, and his naked stomach undulated against Hal's face. His voice was soft but sultry, breathless and with a tortured edge that, to Hal's surprise, sent erotic shock waves straight to Hal's groin. "Put your mouth on me. Slide your hands under my skirt. Oh, Howard, I'm so hot for you—just for you, Howard. I want you to touch me, Howard—*oh!*"

Hal locked his mouth onto Morgan's flat nipple and suckled it hard. Morgan cried out loudly, and Hal slid his hand down around to the back of the skirt. The material annoyed him, so he tucked it into the waistband and slid his hand down the smooth slope of exposed skin, tracing the globe and then sliding back to the heat and the sweet, forbidden crease. The crowd roared, but he heard them only dimly, as if they were very far away.

He trusted that Morgan had some spell around their voices as well—certainly he had one on his own, because he kept shouting Hal's full name, louder and louder, and no one seemed to notice. They did, though, wolf whistle when Morgan, overcome by Hal's torment, slid off his lap, kissed his way down his body, ripped the loincloth-like underwear aside, and took Hal's burgeoning erection in his mouth.

Now it was Hal who cried out. He tried to censor himself, but Morgan had a very talented tongue, and it wasn't long before he was shouting, "Oh, God, *Morgan!*" He pulled Morgan's head closer to push his cock deeper into Morgan's throat and braced his foot on the edge of the chair to allow Morgan better access to the opening his fingers were fumbling insistently for.

The only time Hal came close to shame was when he opened his eyes and saw Eagan watching them. The *laumu* was leaned back in his chair, ankle resting casually on his knee and cigarette balanced gracefully at his fingers as he observed his slave in sexual frenzy. By this time Morgan was on his lap again, his back to Hal, gasping and writhing to the beat as he encouraged Hal's hands over his chest, down his stomach, and beneath his skirt.

Does he know? Hal worried, his fingers faltering at Morgan's thighs. *Does he suspect?* But he couldn't. He would never let this go

148

on. So, that was Eagan, just watching, being really, really creepy. He looked at ease, and quite pleased. *Jesus,* Hal thought. *He's almost getting off on this. What a sick, sick bastard.* He shut his eyes, put Eagan out of his mind, and went back to making love to Morgan.

All the *laumu* were enjoying the performance, it seemed, and they were being awfully accommodating. When the petting began to get serious and even Hal was trying to figure out how to get Morgan onto the floor, they told him to wait and shoved a table closer. When Hal tossed Morgan onto it, someone in the audience shouted, "Tie him down!" and to his shock, Hal found his cock swelling at the thought. Even Morgan seemed to like the idea. And when Eagan ordered rope to be brought for the Hunter, Hal thought, well, he supposed voyeurism was a pretty popular fetish. It made sense with the *laumu.* They struck him as such a nervous, flighty bunch—it had to be easier to watch someone else have sex than to run the risks yourself. Of course, the fact that they thought it was rape was part of their titillation.

I have to get out of here, Hal thought.

He didn't know what Morgan's plan was or if he even had one. For a little while he tried to think of one himself, just in case, but he came to the conclusion that there was no plan to be made. The only options in front of him right now were to make love to Morgan for an audience of enemies or reveal himself as Morgan's inept human lover and be killed. But something was starting to worry him, and it wasn't just his Catholic conscience. He just couldn't figure out what it was.

"Are you sure you're okay with this?" Hal asked Morgan breathlessly as he wrapped the smooth, white rope in the intricate, erotic arrangement around his lover that Morgan himself was dictating. "How is this going to free you?"

"Howard," Morgan replied, pausing to gasp as Hal tugged and forced his shoulders back. He glanced over his shoulder, his eyes bright with lust. "Trust me."

"But how are we going to get away?" Hal asked.

Morgan's bound hands flexed, and for the briefest of moments, Hal saw Shinju's pearl visible in the center of Morgan's left palm. "There is enough magic in this," he said with wicked joy, "to send Los Angeles to the moon. It's what's keeping us disguised, and it's what will free you when I can't stretch this performance out any longer."

"Free *me*?" Hal repeated, pausing. "What about you?"

Morgan gave him a pointed look. "*I* can't leave, obviously, but I can send you far, far away."

Hal tugged tightly on the rope, pulling Morgan's shoulders back again. He ignored the coos of encouragement from the audience and bent forward to speak sternly in Morgan's ear. "I didn't go through all this to get sent away from you again."

"You can't stay," Morgan shot back, in much the same tone. "You shouldn't have come back at all. And you *cannot* come back again. Eagan will be terrible when he finds out how we've tricked him."

"I'm *not leaving you,*" Hal said again, the words coming out almost in a growl. Whatever this translated to the audience, they liked, because they applauded and started calling out "Fuck him! *Fuck him!*" in chorus, until someone hastily amended it to "her."

"I won't let you stay," Morgan shot back. Some of the sexual edge had left him. "You can't stay here if I tell you no."

"I don't see why not," Hal replied, a little more nastily than he meant. He gestured to the crowd. "You don't want *these* assholes in the Oasis, but here they are."

"Howard, please—don't ruin this," Morgan said, his tone softening abruptly. "Please, just make love to me."

It dawned on Hal that, if Morgan could cloak them, alter his appearance, and keep the elixir under control all at the same time, he could even more easily move them into his inner sanctum/safe room. He was *deliberately* keeping them here.

"You really want this, don't you," he said aloud, with no small amount of wonder. "Here, in front of them."

Morgan shifted his body so that he was half turned over and looking at Hal. There was a strange tension in his voice as he spoke. "I have serviced these vermin for well over one hundred years. They have had me in every way possible, in public and private, and they have made certain to humiliate and tease me every time. If they let me enjoy it, they made sure it would be something that made me sick afterwards. They have used me to hurt people and to further their own selfish pursuits. Yes, I want them to see this. I want them to watch what they think is my torment, only to find out in the end that it was nothing but pleasure."

Morgan shuddered and arched as much as the rope would let him as Hal's hand strayed down the slope of his back. "Then I want you to come," Hal said quietly but with force. "I want you to have an orgasm, to climax. With me."

Morgan shook his head urgently. "No, Howard, I told you—it's too dangerous—"

"I want to take the risk." Hal tugged on the rope as he turned Morgan over onto his back. "I want you to be free, Morgan, if only for a minute. And I want you to be free with me."

"It's unnecessary and foolish!" Morgan said, getting angry.

"No more foolish or unnecessary than having sex on stage in front of an audience that thinks you're being raped by your mother's killer!" Hal shot back. He forced himself to calm, and then he reached down to stroke Morgan's cheek. "I will admit, this is a kinky kind of fun, something I wouldn't have expected to enjoy even a little. But it's not why I'm here. I came back to help you, not to give the finger to a bunch of twelve-year-olds. I want to *free you*, Morgan. For good."

"That isn't possible," Morgan said, losing some of his glow.

"I think it might be," Hal replied. "And at the very least, it's worth trying."

He stroked the sides of Morgan's thighs, gentling him as he trembled. "I can't stand to fail again," Morgan whispered at last.

"Then we won't fail," Hal said. He grinned and slid the skirt higher on Morgan's hips, exposing him. "Come on. Let's do our worst."

"Ah, yes," a laconic voice said from the crowd. "Yes—I believe that is quite enough."

Hal stopped, surprised.

Eagan rose and came forward with his hands held up, looking like a parent coming to tell the toddlers that he was through warning them, and now it was time to put the toys away. He nodded to his bodyguards. "Grab him, please."

"What?" This was Morgan, struggling to his elbows, looking around wildly. He looked both angry and afraid. "What is *this*?!"

Eagan gave him a withering look. "*Please,* lover. These idiots might be fooled by illusion, but I am not so green. You and your human have had your fun, and now it is over." When Morgan made a strangled sound, he made a moue with his lips. "Oh, don't pout. You were quite sexy, and I'm sure they're all shocked to find out you were in the throes of true rapture, not rape. See? You won. And now you're done."

That's Eagan for you, Morgan had said, and Hal replayed the whole of the conversation once more in his head now, as he watched his victory turn to ash. *He loves to play games with your head. He loves you to think you're about to get away, only to surprise you at the last second with another length of chain. He enjoys watching hope turn to despair. He thinks it's very funny.*

Hal was still stunned by the turnaround, but the look on Morgan's face made it clear that Eagan had, as far as his prisoner was concerned, lived fully up to form. Morgan was struggling against the ropes, shouting at the bodyguards desperately to *get back*, and Eagan was standing at the perimeter, a lazy smile spreading across his face.

But it was a very small and tentative smile, some part of Hal realized. He'd cut the game off. *He was worried. He was afraid we would go too far.*

He knew that what I was about to try would work.

Hal didn't give himself time to second-guess. As the bodyguards reached for him, he ducked down, jumped onto Morgan, shut his eyes, and reached for the hand he'd seen holding the pearl. He was afraid if he had his eyes open, they would tell him it wasn't there, and then he wouldn't be able to find it, so he groped blindly, and to his relief, when he grabbed Morgan's hand, he found the pearl too.

He snatched it away, rolled off him again, and stood on the table, holding the pearl high above his head.

"Stop right where you are!" he shouted. "Stop, or you'll be sorry!"

It was something of a pathetic shout, but it worked. He suspected it was out of sheer surprise at first, and then because Eagan waved for the men to stand down.

"And why will we be sorry?" he asked, sounding only idly curious for the reply.

"Because if you come any closer, to either of us, I'll smash the pearl." It had been a shot in the dark, but he crowed silently when he saw the flicker of alarm in Eagan's eye. Hal bent his arm and waved the pearl in a gesture he hoped looked ominous. "Can't be good to have so much magic going off in here at once."

Eagan relaxed a little. "That's not what would happen," he said with amused patience.

Shit. So now he had no idea what the pearl would do, and Eagan knew it. Hal tried to counter that failure by giving Eagan a sneering grin. "How do you know what would happen with a human involved?"

A ripple of shock ran through the crowd, and once again Eagan's smug look faded. Hal reached up with his free hand and carefully removed Shinju's earring from his tender ear. He felt the illusion of the Hunter run away from him like water, and when he glanced down at himself, he let out a sigh of relief at the familiar sight of his ragged jeans and worn-out sneakers and plain, pale skin.

"It's him! The *human!*" several *laumu* whispered, in the same voice they might say, "The rabid dog!"

Hal tossed the earring down to Morgan, making sure it landed in his bound hands. Morgan was sitting up now and looking back and forth in confusion between Hal and Eagan.

"I won't let you go," Eagan pointed out. "Not alive. And I won't let you die anytime soon, either. You've become too interesting to kill quickly." He smiled. "Of course, I might be willing to let you leave and take out all my irritation on my lover instead."

"I'm not going anywhere," Hal replied evenly. "It's you who will go. I'm going to cast you out."

Eagan laughed, a full-throated chuckle that quickly spread through the other *laumu*. "Oh, *will* you?" he said before he laughed a little longer before reaching up to wipe his eyes.

"Howard," Morgan called up uncertainly. "Howard, what are you doing?"

"Follow my lead," Hal said and turned back to face Eagan. "Yes, I will. Because I'm going to set Morgan free, right now, in front of you all. I'm going to bring him to a climax, and it will set him free."

Eagan's laughter fell away, but he kept his languid posture. "No," he said, "you won't. And just so you don't get to thinking you're clever, it wouldn't work. It would only blow us all up."

"It *might* blow us all up," Hal corrected. He tried to hide his disappointment, though, because the way Eagan spoke, something made Hal fairly suspicious that Eagan was, in fact, telling the truth. *It's the only game I have,* he decided. *He doesn't want it to happen, so it's the way I have to go.* Hal shifted the pearl in his fingers and smiled. "And I *am* going to do it. And you're going to let me because before I do it, I'm going to let you give me a Stiff Drink."

The crowd hooted, and Morgan roared. "Howard!" he cried, struggling even harder now to free himself. "Howard, *no!*"

But Hal kept his eyes on Eagan, waiting for his reaction. The *laumu*'s eyebrows rose into his hairline, his eyes glittered, and Hal stifled a smile. *Yes,* he thought. *I have you now.*

"Fetch the drink," Eagan said, and the crowd roared.

"Howard!" Morgan was sobbing now. "Howard, you *can't!* I barely saved you the first time! I can't do it now, not with Eagan here to stop me!"

Hal lowered the pearl and looked down at Morgan. Calm. He felt so calm and centered and easy, more than he had ever felt in his whole life.

"It will be all right," Hal told him gently.

"How?" Morgan demanded, tears still running down his face. "*How?*"

"I don't know how just yet," Hal replied, "but I believe with all my heart that this is going to work." And he did. He really did.

Hal laughed and climbed back down off the table. He gathered his half-bound Morgan into his arms and pressed a tender kiss against his lips.

"I don't want to lose you," Morgan whispered and sank against his chest.

"Then don't," Hal replied, stroking his back.

A bodyguard appeared beside him and tapped him on the shoulder. Hal withdrew and saw that the burly man was bearing a silver cup bubbling with a steaming purple liquid inside. He nodded at the man, took the glass from the tray, and raised it to Morgan.

"I know the answer," he said, smiling. "I think I've known it all along, but it wasn't until now that I really understood. He didn't lie to you, Morgan. There really is a prince. There really is a hero. What he didn't tell you was that it is you."

The crowd gasped, Morgan's brows knit together in a frown, and out of the corner of his eye, Hal saw Eagan draw himself upright in alarm.

I was right, he thought. *And now I'm in really big trouble.*

Hal grinned and then lifted the elixir hurriedly to his lips and downed it in one gulp. He tossed the glass to the ground and held his arms out wide.

"Come on, hero," he rasped against his burning throat. "Come and save me."

CHAPTER 8
The Dangerous Human

THE elixir was already starting to affect Hal, but this time he knew what he was up against, and he fought back. It was a little like holding a tidal wave back with an umbrella, but it was something to do while Morgan struggled against his bonds and shouted at him.

"Howard!" he wailed, wriggling and writhing on the table. "Howard, I *can't* save you! You're wrong! I'm not the hero! I'm not *anything!*"

"That's only what he's convinced you to believe," Hal shot back. He swayed on his feet as the potion started to heat him up, but when the bodyguards came closer, he only lifted the pearl up above his head again and tossed them a warning look. Sweat was running down the sides of his face as he turned back to Morgan.

"Think about it, Morgan. You said yourself he likes to tell half-truths and twist things around so that you're damning yourself without knowing it." He shut his eyes as a wave of heat took him, and he reached out for the table to steady himself, bumping his swollen cock against the edge as well. He'd forgotten it was still out of his pants.

He could feel the elixir starting to take him, and he knew he wouldn't be able to speak much longer. So he tried to make his words count.

"You were never his prisoner," he said, his words starting to slur. "He only made you believe you were."

"Howard, it doesn't work like that!" Morgan cried, still fighting the ropes. "He tricked me! He used my own vows against me!"

"He lied!" Hal roared. "It's not true—none of it! That's his game, don't you see? Two thousand years from now, when he's bored with you, he'll set up a fake hero for you, and just when you're walking out the door, he'll say, 'Oh, by the way, you could have left anytime. I just made you think you couldn't.' And then he'll laugh as you crumble in horror, and he'll have won again." Hal hissed as his erection began to turn to pain, but he fought it off as best he could so he could finish. "But I won't let him. I'm a dangerous human, and I'm going to mess everything up as best I can." He shuddered, winced, and then laughed. "One way or the other."

He could tell that Morgan still didn't believe him. He wasn't stunned by Hal's revelation; he was too busy crying and, Hal suspected, imagining what Hal would look like splattered against the walls—*his* walls. Morgan managed to free half of one arm and held out his hand as far as he could. "Give me my mother's pearl," he said, his voice breaking. "I might be able to do something, if I have that."

It was either the magic of the pearl itself or some deep instinct that made him do it, but when Morgan reached for the pearl, Hal snarled, turned, and lobbed it hard and fast at Eagan, who startled but caught it.

"You are the hero!" Hal hissed. He was starting to shake. He was going to fall down any second. He looked up at the walls around him and saw that they were shaking too. Morgan was very, very upset.

Good, Hal thought. Now all he needed to do was listen.

Hal reached out and clutched at him with his fumbling, heavy hands. They were already half numb. "You are the hero," he murmured, through lips that were already swelling shut. "You are your *own hero.* You don't need any magic but your own."

He was aware, dimly, of Morgan shouting and reaching for him as he went down to the ground. But what made him smile as the darkness closed over him was the look of quiet terror he saw on Eagan's face.

HE WASN'T unconscious for long—or at least it didn't feel like long. It was as if, when he fell, his eyes closed in a long blink, and when he opened them, only seconds seemed to have passed, and yet he could tell that far more time had elapsed than that. For starters, he wasn't on the floor but lying across the table. Morgan was bent over him, his face only inches away from Hal's. Hal still felt stiff and swollen, but the worst of it was around his mouth. His mouth felt and tasted awful, like bile. And when he took a closer look at Morgan's mouth, he realized why.

It *was* bile. Morgan had sucked it, and the elixir, out of him.

"Howard," Morgan said, the word itself an expression of relief. He pressed a bile-slimed kiss against his chest. *"Howard."*

Hal saw a shadow move behind Morgan, but before he could even attempt to grunt out a warning, Morgan whipped around, and what looked very much like lightning shot out of his hand.

"Stay back!" Morgan's voice was raw and wild. He had pushed himself up off the table, and he was aiming his palm at them. When it came around toward Hal's face, he could see that Morgan held the fox coin in his hand.

Then Morgan lowered it and bent over Hal again, stroking the sides of his face as he studied his eyes. His shoulders sank.

"I didn't get it all," he whispered. "Not enough."

"You can do it," Hal croaked back. Or tried to. Morgan only looked at him blankly, so he tried to say it in his head.

You can do it. I believe in you.

Morgan's face twisted immediately into tortured agony, and he reached for the lapels of Hal's shirt. "Why, Howard? *Why did you do this?*"

Why do you believe in me?

"I warned you," Eagan's voice called out dryly from the sidelines. "Humans are very unpredictable, and that is why they are so dangerous."

Hal reached up and grabbed Morgan's arm with as much strength as he could. *Tell him,* he all but shouted into Morgan's mind, *to shut the fuck up.* When Morgan only blinked, Hal gripped his arm and said it again. *Tell him to shut the fuck up.*

Without so much as a pause, Morgan turned his head toward Eagan. "Shut the fuck up."

Hal didn't hear Eagan anymore.

161

But he didn't care because he was too busy focusing on Morgan, or trying to. Morgan hadn't done that because he'd wanted to. He'd done it because Hal had given him a command. *He's had a lot of elixir,* he realized. Hal wanted to believe that the elixir was as fake as everything else about Eagan, but he was testament at this very moment that this wasn't the case. But he *knew* he was right about the rest.

So all he had to do was get the elixir out of Morgan and himself without letting anyone else get a shot at a command.

Hal fumbled for Morgan's arm again. He forced himself to say the words out loud, so that they had the best chance of counting— and so that the others heard too.

"Listen," he rasped, "only to me. Obey"—he stopped to brace against a rising wave of pain—"only what I say."

"Oh, *clever*," Eagan snarled from the sidelines. "Goodness, such a shame I never thought of that."

You can't, Hal thought, sliding back along a razor edge of pain. *You can't command him like that.* How did he know that, he wondered? Was he just making it up? Was he getting delirious?

No, the same thought insisted, as the darkness slid over him again. *He can't do that, because it would be against the rules. His rules. And he always plays by the rules.*

Hal didn't know what that meant, and he didn't get a chance to dwell on it further, because the next thing he knew, he had blacked out… and then he was opening his eyes again.

This time he was naked. He was still on the table, but he was naked. He could feel Morgan's mouth on him, and the part of his brain that was forever ready to enjoy sex was purring, but the part of him that wanted to make sure he lived to enjoy sex again was listening and not liking what he *didn't* hear: anything. He didn't hear anything, except the soft, wet sucking at his waist.

Hal turned his head, with great effort, and found himself staring directly at Eagan.

The *laumu* was sitting on a chair, but for the first time in Hal's acquaintance with him, the man was not relaxed. Oh, he was trying to look the part, but anyone who had ever watched a high school or college basketball game knew this pose. Eagan sat on the edge of the chair, his legs spread apart in a position that was supposed to look casual and commanding, but he was leaning forward, too, his elbows braced against his knees, his calves tense, his whole body poised for flight. He was using every ounce of control he had to appear calm and unperturbed, and as a consequence he looked as wound up as— Hal had a brief image of some plastic toy from his youth, a tiny piece of crap with a white knob that turned and turned and turned, and when you let go the little pink mouse crouched down, slower and slower and slower, until, without warning, it sprang backward into a flip and then repeated the move again. Eagan didn't just look ready to flip over. He looked ready to fly.

He wasn't just worried. He was seriously scared.

But he wasn't scared enough, because he wasn't fighting. Which meant Morgan was going about this wrong. Hal sent his mind racing, trying to put himself back on course. Except he didn't know what the course was. He didn't know what to do. He didn't know anything. He was full of poison, and he was going to die, and he hoped to God his mother never found out where, or how—

Hail Mary, full of grace, the Lord is with thee. Blessed art thou among women, and blessed is the fruit of thy womb, Jesus. Holy Mary, Mother of God, pray for us sinners, now and at the hour of our death. Amen.

Hail Mary, full of grace, the Lord is with thee.

Hal didn't know when he'd started saying the prayer, but it was flowing from him now like a fountain. He could feel his lips moving along with the words, and he could feel his mind moving, too, flowing along the old familiar prayer like a river. It made him calm. It made him centered. It made him remember who he was. It made him remember every other time he'd said the prayer—not individually, but all the prayers together, like a great net across his past. He remembered Sister Frances telling him the prayer was like that—that if he said it from his heart, he would not just connect to his own prayers, but to all the other Hail Marys that had ever been spoken from the heart. That this was the way, the true way, to the Virgin and to God. The connection.

The connection.

Hal turned his head back to the ceiling, then reached down, and tugged gently but firmly on Morgan's hair.

"Throw away the medal," he rasped. "Forget about the elixir and make love to me."

"I need the medal to keep them at bay," Morgan protested. "And the elixir—"

"The medal was of St. Thomas," Hal said sharply. "The doubter. You said it had the magic that I put into it. Morgan, I wore that medal like an anchor around my neck as I spent fifteen years second-guessing everything about my life. It was that medal that made me see you falsely. It isn't magic. It's a curse. Throw it away. *Throw it away and use your own magic.*"

He managed the last with enough oomph that it triggered the elixir, and Morgan cried out in despair as the medal ricocheted off into the darkness. And it *was* darkness, Hal realized. All the lights were gone except for an eerie blue glow that surrounded the table.

The Oasis was failing.

Someone tried to rush the table, but without hesitating, Morgan lifted his hand and lashed out again. It wasn't lightning, but it was a pretty intense shaft of wind, and whoever had been rushing wasn't anymore.

"You don't need the medal," Hal said. "And you don't need Eagan. Make love to me, and I'll show you."

"You will *not* take release with this man," Eagan shouted. He sounded very angry. "Not unless you want to see just how angry the San Andreas fault can be."

"He doesn't give a damn about any earthquake," Hal said. He was getting dizzy again, and his cock was swelling. He tried to speak quickly. "You can tell when you're getting close to the way out because he gets testy. He's testy now. You have to do it, Morgan. You have to do it now, before it's too late."

"I can't take the elixir out of you if I do that!" Morgan cried. "Not in time to save you!"

"You don't have any idea what you can or can't do once you aren't under this bastard's influence. I'm willing to take that risk."

"I'm not!" Morgan pressed his hands to Hal's chest. "I don't want you to die! I don't want to lose you!"

"I don't want to live if I have to walk around knowing you're over here with King Asshole making your life a living hell!" Hal felt his jaw start to lock, and he reached up and clutched at Morgan's shoulders. "This is my choice. *My choice.* I can't be your hero. But maybe I can be your light to show you the way to be your own."

It was a very pretty speech, except that it was delivered half-slurred, half-drooled. As Hal finished it, he started to gag and spasm, and his system flooded with adrenaline as his airway started to close.

He heard Morgan cry out as if from very far away. Then he felt his lover move inside him, and Hal smiled or did his best to, and then let go of everything and hoped for the best.

HAL heard Morgan whisper, inside the darkness of his mind, *Hold on, Howard.*

When *he* had come with Morgan inside him, the first time he'd taken the elixir, he'd felt as if he'd splintered into pieces and assembled again back inside his body. As if he had blown out to the edges of a net and then returned. The same thing was happening now, at least in part—when Morgan came, he came, too, and he blew out until he was nothing but tiny bits. Except this time there was no net. This time he kept going and going and going. Hal was lost in darkness with nothing around him, and he realized with cold, stark terror that the danger was not that he might destroy the world, but that he would be lost out here, all alone, forever.

Hail Mary, full of grace, the Lord is with thee—

And then, with no warning, there was a jolt and a snap. There was a tightening—resistance—a pull like nothing Hal had ever felt, as if he'd been stretched to the edge of himself and then stretched further and rolled as thin as paper. He had been blown out into outer space, and there he was, himself, in the middle of nowhere.

And all around him was Morgan.

He could see him here, truly see him in a way he could never see him anywhere else, he realized. Not in the world. Morgan truly was a *place*, and he was large and beautiful and powerful. It was as if Hal were in the center of a great net, a suspension of stars. All that was around him and in him and of him was Morgan. They were as

166

joined as they could be without merging: wholly joined, not Morgan's projected image, but his true self, strange and unreal and magical and beautiful. So, so beautiful.

I'm here, Howard, Morgan said, and Hal shivered as he felt a huge, invisible hand stroke first one side and then the other of his body. *I'm here with you.*

Hal grinned, not looking anywhere in particular, because he knew that everything around him was his lover. "We're here together," he pointed out.

Your body, Morgan said, sounding tense. *Your body still has the elixir inside of it.*

Hal looked down at himself. He felt fine. He looked *great,* actually. Then he wondered, was he actually here? Was this his body or his mind? He had no idea. It felt like a body, but something told him this was a place where you didn't dare assume anything.

"I feel okay," he ventured at last.

You have to go back, Morgan said, less panicked, but still concerned. *I think I can take it out from here, but first you have to go back. I don't want to hurt you by accident.* Another stroke against Hal's body. *I don't want to hurt you ever again.*

"You've never hurt me," Hal insisted.

I hurt you when I sent you away, Morgan pointed out.

Hal considered this. "You didn't mean to hurt me. You meant to protect me. In my book, that doesn't count."

Morgan laughed, a musical chuckle that danced around Hal's ears like a fountain. *I like your book.*

"I like you," Hal replied, grinning, and then sobered a little as he added, "I love you, Morgan. Not what you are. Not what you can do. Not how good you are in bed, though—" He blushed and then grinned again. "I just love you. I loved you too soon and too fast and too deep, in a way that doesn't make sense and never will. My love isn't rational, Morgan. That means I'll never stop trying to find you if I lose you. I'll never stop. Ever." He tensed a little and added, "That means that if you don't come back with me, you had damn well better come back soon."

I have to make sure I'm truly free of him before I can return. I have to make sure I have undone all the spells he cast around me, real and imagined, so that when I come back to you, I am well and truly free. Hal felt him hesitate, and then he could feel the gentle blush and tenderness in Morgan's heart as he added, *And I love you too.*

Except, Hal realized, that Morgan would always be willing to let him go if he thought it would be better for him.

Well, Hal thought to himself as he felt himself sliding back down to earth, *every couple needs something to fight about.*

HAL felt the world shift and change, and then he felt his body, and then he felt the pain. He could not move. Not an eyelash, not a finger. He could not breathe, and he got the terrible feeling that he hadn't been breathing for some time. *I'm going to die,* he thought, with a strange calm.

And then he felt lightning go through him, and he gasped, and he shuddered, and he came so hard he was fairly sure he'd lifted briefly off the table.

Hero

Sorry, he heard Morgan's voice whisper in his ear. *It took a second to figure out how to do it from here. But it's all out of you now.*

Hal blinked and let out a shuddering sigh of relief as he realized that he could move again. He wiggled a little more, carefully, just to be sure, and then he sat up slowly and looked around.

He was naked, and he was surrounded by the *laumu*.

They had transformed themselves again, but now they were not men or women: they were horrible, ghastly, ghoulish things like demons and wraiths. Hal felt small and vulnerable enough in the *laumu*'s presence when they were beautiful, but this was worse, and being naked didn't help. There were no more walls, no more anything around him but the monsters, who looked like every bad dream he'd ever had in his life. He even thought he recognized a few of them. Add in the fact that he was naked and still sore and swollen from the elixir, and it was a very close approximation to his childhood imaginings of hell. And even some of his adult imaginings too.

Morgan is here somewhere, Hal told himself. *And he will come back.* Hal slid off the table, and he stood, tall and strong, waiting for whatever was to come.

Eagan stepped forward from the crowd, looking very angry. He looked nightmarish, too, like the gaunt rent boy again but even leaner. The hollows of his cheeks were sunken, his mouth too long and lined with strings of saliva as he spoke.

"So. You set him free. *Clever boy.*" Eagan sneered, and the lines of saliva shivered. "You will pay dearly for that."

He motioned to the bouncers, who came forward with heavy chains, their cuffs opened and ready. Eagan watched, no longer languid, just gleeful as they shackled Hal. Hal, being naked and tired and still shaken by the images around him, didn't resist.

"He is gone, but you are not, human, and now you are mine. You are mine for a long, long time." He leered in the darkness, and Hal couldn't help it. He shivered. The catlike Eagan had been creepy but mostly annoying. This Eagan was harder to fight.

Because he is playing off your fears, now, that thinking voice inside him whispered. *Morgan fears indifference. You fear damnation and shame.*

"You will wish for death many times, human," Eagan was saying, "before I am done with you. I will keep you alive for years beyond what a human should live, and I will visit you with pain beyond what you can even dream."

Hal held himself still, not letting Eagan see his fear. "Morgan escaped," he said, as if to say that this was worth it. "He made it out of your prison." He tried to add *and so will I,* but he didn't think he could pull it off.

It pleased him that this only made Eagan angrier, but he didn't like the smug look that replaced the anger. The *laumu* came closer, closing the distance between them.

"Morgan made his own prison, you fool, just as you will." Eagan ran a fingernail down Hal's cheek and then turned it and cut sharply against the skin, making Hal wince and suck in a breath. Eagan smiled. "But that's the game, you see? I can turn your life into whatever hell it is you feel you deserve. I can see all the way into your soul. *You* are now my prisoner. There's no way out of here without him. And if he comes back, I'll recapture him too. One way or another, boy, you're here forever." He lifted his finger and licked the blood off the tip, and grinned. "You are *mine*."

Eagan reached out and stroked Hal again; Hal stiffened and turned his face away. Eagan laughed.

"Oh, the fun we will have," he purred. "It was always a bit distasteful to rape Morgan, knowing he enjoyed it, but you won't like it. That will be nice." Eagan grinned. "I hope the world never runs out of tender-hearted idealists like the pair of you. It is so very delicious to destroy your illusions. We will begin now." He came very close to Hal, his dark eyes dancing with an unholy light.

Hal should have been miserable, or at the very least terrified. But somehow he wasn't. He was scared and nervous, but it was like standing at the edge of a diving board. All you had to do was jump, and it would be over. Morgan *wasn't* trapped. Morgan *would* find a way out. He knew it with his very soul. He was here, listening; Hal could feel him.

He could feel him everywhere.

"He didn't love you, you know," Eagan was saying. "He couldn't. I took that from him first, a long time ago. At best he feels longing for you, but it isn't the same." Eagan looked thoughtful and tapped a gaunt cheek. "Oh, my—I wonder if he *will* come back, then, at all?"

Hal frowned at Eagan and then raised an eyebrow. "That's it? That's your opening shot? That Morgan doesn't love me?"

Eagan gave him a pitying look. "Oh dear. Did he convince you that he did? I'm *so* sorry." He shrugged. "Well, you'll find out soon enough, I suppose."

Hal almost laughed. It would have been a great blow—three days ago. It was the sort of thing that would have had him all self-conscious and doubting. But not now. Not after what he'd just seen and felt with Morgan—*in* Morgan.

171

Eagan watched him carefully, seemed to dislike what he saw, then took another shot. "Your mother will be very disappointed when she finds out what your life was really like in Los Angeles. All those drugs and the dirty whores."

Okay, *that* one struck a mark, but it pissed him off more than anything else. Hal aimed an angry finger at him. "You shut up about my mother. You can't touch her. Shinju saw to that."

Eagan laughed, and the sound made Hal shudder. "You *believed* her?"

"I did," Hal shot back, but with a little less confidence than he'd have liked. He tried to recover and added, "I *do.*"

"And you honestly think the queen of the *kitsune* will go all the way to Kansas to make sure I don't 'bother' some worthless woman who doesn't even rule the local women's guild?" Eagan rolled his eyes to the ceiling and shook his head in weary disbelief. Then he held out his arms and looked at Hal. "Where are they now, Hal? Where is your lover? Where is his mother?" The pearl appeared in Eagan's hand, and he handed it to Hal with a sneer. "Here—you were so eager to work its magic before. Why don't you call her? Bring her to us, and let her answer for you."

Hal clutched the pearl in his hand tightly, but he did nothing. He was losing the edge here. He wasn't sure he'd ever had it. He tried to keep himself calm, and he tried to have faith, but it was getting hard.

Hurry up, hero, he tried to whisper to Morgan. *I could use some saving here.*

But the words went nowhere, and even as he felt doubt and panic searching for purchase inside him, he knew the true answer was that this was *his* moment to play hero to himself. Funny how he was so sure that Morgan could do it, so sure he'd risk his own life to help him see. Funny how now, when all he had to do was not listen to the asshole in front of him, he was drowning before he started.

A crowd of *laumu* had circled around them, a huge crowd—the entire population of them, it seemed, had come, and they watched as their leader taunted their new toy. Eagan was leering now.

"Oh, the things you want, Hal Porter—they're shameful things. You've tried so hard to keep yourself from sin, but all you've done is put it off, haven't you? You still want it all, because deep down, you know you're nothing but a bad, bad man."

Hal gave him a funny look. "You're trying to sell guilt to a Catholic? You really don't know much about humans."

"I know *all* about humans," Eagan replied, not missing a beat. "Wild and strange. Beasts without laws, so you make your own. You have no king, no queen, no god, no country, and so you invent them all. You make your own heavens, and you make your own hells." His smile was terrible, and Hal recoiled as he ran a skeletal finger down his cheek. "You need no masters, but you crave them. You are more easily led than sheep. Oh, you'll fight me for awhile. But you are easy. You need simple things like food and water and sleep. It won't take much to make you into the most tender of playthings. Morgan has done us all a favor, really."

And yet he thinks that humans are dangerous. Hal pushed his fear aside and looked Eagan in the eye. "So what are *your* laws, Eagan?" When Eagan's eyes narrowed, Hal pressed on. "Wait, don't tell me. I'll guess." He studied the *laumu*'s face and tried to remember what he already knew. "You have to play by the rules, that I know. Whatever your rules are, you can't break them. Ever. You can put whatever chains you want on others, but they're nothing compared to those that hold you down."

"Oh, *so clever,*" Eagan said but too softly.

"And I know you're nothing more than a parasite," Hal went on, not sure where he was pulling all this from but riding it all the way to the end of the line. "You *need* someone to bully, to abuse. If you don't have a host, you're nothing." He looked again at their gaunt, terrible bodies, and suddenly it all made sense. "Also, right now, you're weak. If you really wanted to scare me, you'd have become a bunch of nuns or, worse, frat boys and sorority girls. But you can't manage that yet, so you're going with nightmares. You're weak, because Morgan has left as much as he can leave, and you're floundering. You only have the shell of what he has left. You're trying to find purchase in me, and I'm not going to let you. You can wither and die where you stand."

He was talking fast now, a little nervous, a little excited, and a little impatient. *Morgan, where the hell are you?*

Somehow Eagan caught that thought, and he seized on it. "Yes—where *is* my little lover? Why isn't he coming to save you?"

"He'll be along," Hal said with calm confidence. But Eagan caught the fear that lurked underneath as easily as catching a leaf drifting on the wind.

"But he might not be strong enough yet to save you," Eagan finished for him out loud.

Hal shrugged. "Then we'll defeat you together. If not today, then tomorrow."

"So brave," Eagan said, with mock admiration. "And such a fool. You believe in his love, don't you? A love you've known for a scant handful of days. The love of a man, the sort of love you weren't willing to accept even a week ago. Are you certain you want to bank everything on *this?*"

"Yes," Hal said, and his voice was strong and sure. "I love Morgan, and that's all I need. I'm not like you—I don't need his love in return to make me okay. I can do that on my own."

And there it was. Hal saw the words strike hard at the center of Eagan, and he saw that they were true. For one moment, he knew pity. Then he remembered what Eagan had done, and what he had promised to do, and he pushed on.

"Loving Morgan makes me feel whole." Hal kept his gaze level and his shoulders square. "My whole life, I've just been empty, wandering through, not really living. I've been good as I could be, but it was just holding back. I tried to deny who I was and what I wanted, and I let the fear of what accepting myself might do rule me. I tried to hide. I tried not to think about the emptiness. I tried to fill it with working and books and church and silence. I've tried it all, but nothing ever worked. And yet, though in the past twenty-four hours I've lost my job, been kidnapped, raped, abused, used, terrified, humiliated, and nearly killed... somewhere in the middle of all that, I fell in love. I don't know why or how, and I don't care. I just know that I did, and that in that moment, I was more alive than I've been in thirty-two years of living. It wasn't Morgan's love that saved me. It was giving up my fear and loving him first. *That's* my heaven, Eagan, and it's my hell too. But it's *mine*. And it's somewhere I will never, ever let you go."

Hal stopped, breathless, exuberant, and victorious. The *laumu* had gone completely still, and Eagan, looming over Hal, was red-faced with rage. But Morgan still was not here. Eagan was. And even though he saw that he had seen the truth of what the *laumu* were, he saw, too, that this did not make them impotent, not by a long shot.

"I will ask you," Eagan growled, "in ten years if you still think that I cannot give you hell." He raised his hand above his head, a long, wicked-looking knife appearing in his grip. "In honor of your sickening little love, then, the first part of you I will destroy will be your heart."

You will not touch him.

Eagan stopped. Hal stopped. Everyone turned, looking for the voice, but there was no one. It had boomed out as if it were the voice of God, distorted, angry, and heavy, sinking down over the dark void that was what was left of the Oasis and settling in their hearts. A cold wind had whipped up around the words, but now that they were spoken, the wind was gone. The crowd began to whisper, crouching nervously, but nothing else came. Eagan glanced around once more, making certain, and then set his jaw and raised his knife again.

The wind was back before Eagan even finished raising the blade again. *You will not harm the one I love.*

This time when the voice boomed, the earth shook too—and this time, though it was still distorted, Hal knew the voice. Eagan did too. And unlike Hal, who felt his heart lift and expand inside his chest, Eagan lowered the knife and turned an angry face to the sky.

"You left, you ungrateful little worm!" he shouted. He grinned a dark grin and came to stand behind Hal, gripping him by the back of his hair, yanking him back against his chest. "*He* is mine now. You *left*. He gave you your release, and now he is here in your place."

He is not yours to take, Morgan said. His voice was still inside the great wall of sound, but it was as if he had suddenly become much, much more. It shook the earth, and Hal, and his chains, and then suddenly, his chains were gone.

But Eagan kept his hold on him.

"If you want to come back in his place, I would be happy to make a trade," Eagan said silkily.

"No!" Hal shouted and then winced as Eagan hauled him back again.

A great, thick, angry bolt of lightning struck the ground, hitting the place where Eagan had been standing just moments ago; Hal could smell the burning ground in its wake. The crowd cried out and shrank back, but Eagan didn't so much as flinch.

"Ah, ah, ah," Eagan scolded. "If you want him, sweetheart, you're going to have to come and get him."

Dark clouds had formed above, and they were billowing low. Lightning crackled within them, but no more bolts came down to strike the ground.

Is that an invitation, Eagan? Morgan asked, a clap of thunder capping the end of his words.

Eagan leaned forward and laved his long, black tongue across Hal's cheek. "Lover, it's a *challenge*."

A strange, dark laugh bellowed out from the clouds. *Good,* Morgan said.

And then the sky exploded.

CHAPTER 9
hero

IT BEGAN with a sonic boom. Hal had only heard one once, at an Air Force base in Colorado, but that jet's takeoff had nothing on this. The crack seemed to come from inside his body, and he rocked from the force of it; he would have fallen to the ground if Eagan hadn't held him upright. The rest of the *laumu* did fall over, and some of them were trying to crawl away, though where they thought they were going, Hal had no idea. He hadn't ever been aware of the borders of the Oasis, but suddenly he was, and it was not, he realized, that large. They were all trapped here, in fact, in a very close space.

If Eagan felt the shift, he didn't seem to care. He jerked Hal's head back again and shouted up at the sky. "You can't come back, lover," he taunted, "not unless you come back as my slave. You know the rules."

Yes, I know the rules. They are important. Rules are very important, Morgan's voice boomed out again, though it was quieter now and more thoughtful. *I heard what you said to Howard about them, and I heard what he said to you. I have been quiet, you see, not because I have been afraid or because I did not love Howard, but because I have been trying very hard to remember what it was you said to me when you tricked me into letting you in. Because I'm going to use the rules, Eagan, to send you away.*

Hal felt Eagan's grip on him tighten and then deliberately slacken. "Will you, now? Very well—this should be amusing for a few moments. Let's hear what you've discovered."

The winds shifted gently around them. *You told me that you loved me and that you would always care for me. I used to think that you lied. But you didn't, did you? You "loved" me and "cared" for me as much as you were able. Which wasn't much at all. But you did keep your word.*

"And if you recall, you promised to love me in return and care for me and keep me safe. Forever. How, lover, do you plan to get out of that?"

Eagan's voice had turned silky and bored again, Hal noticed. He was like a chameleon, changing to become the sort of incubus most suited to whomever he was stalking.

Very easily, Morgan said. *I must only be as true to my promise as you have been to yours. What you need and what I need are not in harmony, but at odds. You can never love or care for me as I need. And therefore, I need not love or care for you as you need. In fact, as you well know, I will never survive if I continue to try.*

"You overlook one crucial point," Eagan shot back, speaking against the wind, which was growing stronger now. "You granted me access to the Oasis—you granted me *control* of the Oasis. You can hide in your corner if you like, but I won't leave, and *you* don't have what it takes to kick me out." He grinned at the sky. "You'll get lonely, lover. You always do. You'll come out, and I'll be cruel, and you'll be sad, and so I'll give you more elixir to make the pain go away."

It's true, Morgan conceded. *I cannot evict you. But you are wrong in saying I gave you control of me. I* lent *you control of me. That I did not swear by, and so I can take it back. But you are deliberately misunderstanding me, I think. I am not saying I am evicting you. I am saying that I will not love you any longer. And, perhaps more importantly to you, I am saying that I will not protect you.*

Eagan stopped smiling.

Hal felt the ground beneath his feet begin to shift, and even though the world was still dark, he could feel the walls of the Oasis closing in around them.

The Oasis has been destroyed—by you, Eagan, and your coldness and your greed. I must start again. I must build it again. We have done this before, of course, because you have hurt me this much before. But this time will be different. I will not shelter you in a foolish hope that this time you might learn to love me. This time you will be on your own.

Hal winced as Eagan seized him by the neck and did a fair job of hauling him off the ground. "And what of this one? Will you destroy him too? Or will you make him an exception? *That* is against the rules."

No, it isn't, Morgan said, but Hal noticed he was not quite as composed this time. *But even so, I can't have you trying to tag along with him, which I know you will. And so I have made it an open exception. I will protect anyone in the Oasis who can find their way to my heart. Find me there, and I will shelter you.*

Hal was surprised to hear Eagan laugh—long and hard.

"Oh, lover," Eagan purred. "You will regret this one. To set such a task before a human? And for *this* one?" He held up something that flashed, and then he tossed the fox coin to Hal—

180

except that, once more, it was St. Thomas on a chain. "There go you, Doubter. I'd hate to think you went on your quest unarmed."

He laughed again and ran off into the darkness, leaving Hal alone.

The whole ground was shaking, far worse than any earthquake Hal had experienced. The *laumu* around him were shrieking and running, some occasionally stopping to fall to the ground and clutch at their heads, but some just kept running. They seemed to see and feel something different than Hal. They were reacting to things Hal couldn't see or feel. The only thing Hal knew was that, if there were walls, they would soon be falling down around him.

But he soon realized the walls weren't falling. They were rising up out of the ground.

They were *strange* walls. They looked like something out of a fairytale, all stone and vine and curving arch, and they'd have been something to see if they weren't trying to knock him over or come up through his leg. Now he was running, too, but the walls were coming up everywhere, no rhyme or reason at all. Two came up at once, and Hal was nearly smashed between them as they fused together.

"Morgan!" Hal cried. He quickly put the medallion around his neck and tried to find safe ground. There wasn't any. "Morgan, I can't find you!"

You can, Morgan whispered urgently. *You can find me, Howard. I have brought you to where I am before. You can find it again, but you have to open your eyes.*

"Trust me, I have them open!" Hal shouted, and then he leaped off an edge that was threatening to carrying him up toward the ceiling. He ended up on another one heading to the same place.

There was hardly any space left on the ground now. The Oasis was now a world of walls.

Maybe you should close them, then, Morgan suggested. He was starting to sound worried. *Hurry, Howard—I can't stop this, now that I've started it. And it's true. If I pluck you out, he will follow you. And I can't let him in here anymore, not after having you. I would never survive.*

"He's run off!" Hal clutched at a pillar as it carried him up, but it was swelling, and soon he couldn't hold onto it at all. He clung to the ivy instead, but it was groaning, ready to break.

He's right behind you. I can see what you can't see, Howard. You are so close to the door. It is just before you. All you have to do is step out, and walk into it.

"Morgan, if I step out, I'm going to fall to my death! I'm not built to survive that!"

All you have to do is step out, Morgan repeated. *I cannot tell you any more.*

He went quiet, and Hal was left alone, grabbing at new ivy as old gave way, falling and rising at the same time. The walls were becoming slick, too, and the ivy was starting to fall apart. There wasn't mental room for a Hail Mary here. He was going to have to suss this out on his own.

All he had to do was step out. Except that he'd die if he did. Was this like Indiana Jones, and he just had to step out and the bridge would appear?

You have been here before, Morgan had said. *You know the way.*

Maybe you should close your eyes.

182

Hal did.

And he saw.

It was faint. It was confusing. But he definitely saw something, in the same way he had seen the bar and seen the pearl. He saw the glass palace. He was *in* the glass palace. *Sand.* The stones were made of sand, and they were fusing together, packing one on top of another, harder and faster and tighter, and the heat and the pressure were making glass.

In his vision, the prince had been in the tower. Keeping his eyes closed, Hal tipped his head up.

"Step *out?*" he called into the wind and noise of smashing walls. "You're sure you don't mean *up?*"

You're so close, Morgan whispered. *Does it really matter which way?*

Hal looked down at the ground, which he couldn't see because of all the smashing sand. "It's a pretty important difference." The ivy he was holding onto began to give. He opened his eyes and looked around in the way that mattered to his body, and he realized that there was only one way to go up now—but all those rides were razor-sharp edges of glass. Clearly, it was time for a little more thinking.

He went somewhere Eagan couldn't reach him and couldn't go. *His heart. Morgan's heart.* With Morgan, that wouldn't be something soft and squishy that beat inside his chest. It would be the heart of a place. A house. A kitchen? No. His heart. It was where he kept his heart.

His room.

His room, without doors or windows, that even for Morgan took some effort to get inside.

"I have it," he said, hanging on just one vine now. "I think. I'm going to try."

Hurry, Howard! Morgan cried.

"If I screw this up," Hal shouted, trying not to let his panic get the better of him, "it doesn't change the fact that I love you. It just means I'm a little slow. Remember that."

Howard!

His vine broke. But Hal let go before he fell, closed his eyes, and stepped out—

—and into Morgan's room.

It didn't feel like anything at all. It felt like moving through a wisp of fog. Even a veil would have been heavier. It *had* been right there, and all around him.

Because Morgan had invited him into his heart. Because he had been, actually, already there all along. And to put his body there, all he had to do was know that and believe.

Morgan was here, too, perched very still and quiet at the edge of his bed.

Hal looked at him, and he could barely breathe. Morgan was sitting there, flesh and blood, yes, looking very much the same and yet like nothing Hal had ever seen. He was shining softly like a sun. His skin was white and pure; his hair, still black, was ringed with light; and from the center of his body came a bright white pulse that warmed Hal and gave him an ease like nothing he'd ever known. It was as if the sun itself had come down and was standing before him. Morgan had been beautiful to him in all his forms, but this was beyond anything Hal could comprehend.

He stumbled back and found himself supported by one of the walls. "Wow," was all he could manage. Then he got a better look at Morgan's face, and he started forward. "Hey," he said gently. "It's okay. I'm here. It's okay."

"It was so hard," Morgan whispered. "It was so hard to sit here and know that, if you couldn't find me, I'd end up here all alone. Again." He wiped the tears away from his eyes. "I should be glad to be rid of them. But you don't know what it's like to be so big and so different. I'm lonely *all the time.* Even being with people who hated me was better than being all by myself." He looked at one of the walls, and Hal could tell that he was seeing through them to what was going on outside. "They're dying. Thousands of them. Some will live, and they will come back like ghosts. And *he* is still out there. He will always be there, reminding me." He drew his knees to his chest. "Oh, Howard. I should not be sad. But I am."

Hal sat down beside Morgan. He was still naked, but he held the St. Thomas medal in one hand and the pearl in the other. He set them on the bed behind them, reached out, and drew Morgan carefully into his arms.

"Fill yourself up with new people. Better people." He kissed Morgan's temple. "It won't take much to improve."

"But how can anyone love me?" Morgan whispered, sinking onto his shoulder. "I am so strange."

"You are wonderful," Hal corrected him. "You are the most amazing, wonderful man I've ever known."

Morgan nuzzled his face into Hal's neck and kept it there. "You risked your life for me. So many times."

"I'd do it again," Hal said.

Morgan lifted his head and kissed him, softly. "Will you stay with me, Howard? Will you stay with me always?" Before Hal could answer, Morgan went on. "I didn't lie to Eagan. I do need someone. You said your love for me was enough to make you strong. But I'm not like that. It has something to do with being too big. I needed my mother to guide me when I was small, and I need a mate to guide me now that I am grown. Someone to help keep me from being lost." He fumbled against Hal's naked thigh and found his hand. He ran his fingernail along his palm, making concentric circles across it. "Someone to love me."

Hal watched Morgan's pale hand move against his own. "Are you asking me to marry you?" he asked, quietly, when he was able.

"Yes." Morgan stroked the inside of Hal's palm a while and then, as if he had worked to gather his courage, lifted his head. "Will you?"

Hal smiled, and he felt as if his whole body was smiling too. "I will," he said. He kissed his lover full and hard on the mouth.

Morgan made a soft sound of joy into his mouth and tossed him backward onto the bed, falling after him and sliding his hands over Hal's stomach as his mouth made its way down the center of his chest. But something hard poked Hal in the center of his back, and he gently nudged Morgan away so he could prop himself on his elbow and pull out the pearl. He held it in his hand for a moment and looked up at Morgan.

"I'm not the only one who loves you, Morgan." He handed the pearl to him.

Morgan held it uncertainly in his hand. "I sent her away. I sent them all away."

"They would come back. At the very least, *she* would." Hal nudged him gently. "Try to call her now." Morgan bit his lip, and then he nodded and held the pearl away from him. Just in time, Hal looked down at himself and added quickly, "Ah, Morgan, do you have any spare clothes?"

Morgan smiled at him, a little wickedly. He put the pearl aside and ran a finger along Hal's chin. "Will you think I am strange if I tell you that I enjoyed making love with you in front of people?" The finger traced Hal's lips, and then his thumb tugged briefly on the flesh to part them. "That I would like, in fact, to do it again?"

"I don't think I could do it in front of your mother," Hal confessed. Then he shut his eyes and turned his face into Morgan's palm. "But yes, I liked it too. Except for the part where they wanted to kill me."

"You were wrong," Morgan said, still stroking him softly. "I may have had to save myself, but you're still my hero. And I will be grateful that you found me until the end of time." He stroked Hal's chest. "Which—I should perhaps point out—if you marry me, you will be around to see."

Hal raised an eyebrow at him. "How is that, exactly?"

"That might be a question better asked of another." He pulled the pearl back out and sighed. He reached out and touched Hal's leg again, and as he did so, Hal was once again wearing the same jeans and T-shirt he'd had on beneath the Hunter's disguise. He felt plain next to Morgan in his silken robes, but Morgan didn't seem to care. He was too fixated on the pearl in his hand.

Hal picked up his medal, reached over, and clasped the chain around Morgan's neck.

"I don't need it anymore," Hal said. "But you can use it to remember what we've been through together and how I'll always come home to you. Always." He took Morgan's hand and squeezed it tight. "Now call your mother."

Morgan held the pearl out before him, shut his eyes, and blew a short, soft breath across its surface.

The pearl dissolved like dust, and when it settled down again, Shinju, dressed all in white and missing part of her right arm, was standing before them.

IT PAINED Hal to see that missing arm. It didn't seem to bother Shinju at all, and he knew if he asked her about it, she would scoff and say that she would have given up far more for her son. But he couldn't shake the guilt that, if he had been a little braver or a little more clever, she might have been able to keep it.

Morgan saw it, too, and Hal could tell he was feeling much the same way. But unlike Hal, he did not simply wallow in his guilt; he reached out, took his mother's stub, and ran his hand down the place where her hand should be. And just like that, it was back and she was whole again.

"It won't travel outside the Oasis with you," Morgan said sadly. "But it will be just like the arm you gave up for me while you are here."

Shinju put both her hands on his shoulders, regarded him a moment, and then drew him close to her breast. "Sora. Morgan. My sweet, dear son."

She spoke softly for several minutes in Japanese, and Morgan whispered back in kind. Hal felt like a bit of a voyeur, but it was so beautiful he could not look away, caught up in the sight of their long-awaited embrace. It made him homesick, too, for *his* mother. And as he watched them reunite, he thought, *I have to go home as soon as this is settled.* He wished he could take Morgan, too, but obviously he couldn't.

The wedding would have to be here too. He hoped his mother would come. But where would she stay? Come to think of it, where would *he* stay? Was he still wanted by the police? He didn't have a job. What was he going to do now?

Hal began to fidget on the bed. He reached into his jeans for the coin and then up to his neck to touch his medal, remembered where it was now, and lowered his hand. He stood up, put his hands into his pockets, and waited.

When Shinju and Morgan finally pulled away from one another, Hal looked up and saw that they were no longer in Morgan's room but back on the plane of the Oasis. The walls had stopped rising and stood like strange sentries around them. In the distance there were scuttling sounds, and Hal realized this was the last of the *laumu*, trying to hide.

"The others want to see you too," Shinju said to Morgan. "But they will wait, if you are not ready."

Morgan looked surprised. "But—but it has been so long, and I was so terrible!"

Shinju smiled. "Darling, they were young, too, once. And there are new *kitsune* you have not met who are eager to meet my son." Her eyes glittered as she added, "And all of them are eager to help you clean up any lingering debris that might remain."

Morgan's face shadowed. "Eagan is still here. You won't be able to hurt him."

"Oh, I wouldn't dream of it," Shinju said silkily. "But he will be very hungry very soon. And it has been so long since I have had a servant." That got a smile out of Morgan, and Shinju winked at Hal. "Come, my son. Open your heart to the others, so they may join us in planning the celebration for your return—and, if I understand the look between the two of you, your upcoming wedding."

Morgan rolled his eyes heavenward as he turned to Hal, but he was smiling. "She was *always* like this," he said, without any real complaint. "So bossy." Morgan touched Hal on the shoulder. "Are you all right?"

Hal nodded. "I'm just—it's a little overwhelming." He looked around at the towers of glass and the ivy littered on the ground.

"There are some details," Shinju said, "that I suspect my son has not thought to tell you, as he doesn't understand the needs or composition of the rest of us. But you will alter now, Howard. You will enjoy some freedom before the wedding, but even then you will not be able to go very far and not for very long. Once you join with Morgan, you will be even more limited. He will fade and dissemble if you go too far. And you will live as long as he does, which as far as you can conceive, will seem like forever."

Hal felt uneasy, but he tried not to let Morgan see. "Can I—will I still have a job? What about money?" *What about my mother?*

"Howard—" Morgan took his hand. He looked puzzled. "I can give you anything you will ever need."

Shinju spoke before Hal could figure out how to answer. "My son, your lover is human now. He will require things you cannot give or even see or understand." She turned back to Hal. "There are ways to work around the limitations. Do not fear. I will help you navigate them, if you like."

But what about my mother? Hal wanted to ask, but Shinju had turned back to Morgan and was speaking in Japanese again. He tried to calm himself down. Obviously Shinju would make sure he could see his mother. She understood about mothers. But the trouble was that the same old obstacles to his mom's coming to Los Angeles were still there, and now they were even worse. Hal couldn't imagine leaving Morgan, even for this. But the idea that he couldn't see his mother again, ever, cast a shadow over his happiness.

"It is time," Shinju said in English, and Morgan nodded and stepped forward into the center of the plane, raising his hands to the sky. His hands glowed white and shot beams of light up into the clouds. The light faded—and the sky filled with foxes.

They were like clouds rushing down to earth, brown and silver and white and gold, foxes of all sizes and colors, some with one tail, some with two, three, or four, and some as many as nine. A few of the remaining *laumu* came screaming out of the darkness, but as soon as they were visible, the *kitsune* rushed at the *laumu*, snarling and snapping. And as the *laumu* ran, each one of them changed, and Hal saw that every one of them was nothing more than a tiny green pixie, small and slight and ugly. He saw, for the first time, a few Hunters, too, but though they were large and dangerous, they were no match for the horde of foxes that descended upon them.

Morgan came up beside Hal, took his hand, and together they watched the last of the *laumu* go down.

When it was over, a fox ran up to Morgan; as it came to a stop, it changed into a handsome, middle-aged Japanese man and bowed. "The *laumu* are gone, my lord."

Morgan turned to Hal, smiling. "Would you like to help me build a new palace?"

Hal laughed and started to reply, but then he saw Shinju coming toward them, and he faltered.

"You *are* troubled," Morgan said, squeezing his hand. "What is wrong?"

Hal turned away from Morgan's mother, but his heart was still heavy. "I want to stay with you," he said, "but there is just one problem."

"Whatever it is, we will fix it," Morgan said, determined.

But Hal only shook his head and frowned at his feet. "It's complicated," he said, "and it's not something you can fix."

"I told you," Shinju said, coming up beside them, "that I will help you." She kissed her son on the cheek and then turned and kissed Hal as well. Then she turned to the fox soldier standing at attention beside Morgan. "How far is it to Kansas?"

CHAPTER 10
The Oasis

"ONCE again," Gerry said as Hal took the seat he offered him, "I can't say 'I'm sorry' enough." He shook his head. "I should have listened to those rumors about Todd. It's bad enough he was embezzling from the main company—but then to have him blame you for it! And then that shit with the cops and that freaky guy at your house. He's nuts, man. Completely crazy."

"Again, I'm not worried about it. I have bigger things to worry about right now." Hal leaned back in the chair and threaded his fingers over his stomach. "How's the reconstruction going?"

"Good, good. I'm almost glad for the earthquake, these new plans are so good." He gave Hal a look over the top of his half-glasses. "I hear a rumor the designs are *yours*."

"Mine and my partner's." Hal reached into his pocket and pulled out an envelope. "Speaking of which, I'm going to be busy for a few weeks, so you'll want to speak directly to the chief investor from now on."

Gerry's face lit up as he took the envelope. "So I finally get to meet your boss, double agent?" He frowned at the page he opened. "Shin-what?"

"Shinju. And I told you, I'm not a company spy. She's my mother-in-law, or she's about to be. It just made more sense to her for me to do the back and forth with you while she was away."

Gerry laughed. "You old dog! You're marrying the investor's daughter!"

Hal paused only a moment. "Son, actually."

There was a silence that went on a little too long, and Hal was tempted to blush and clear his throat, but he just sat there calmly and waited for Gerry to process what he'd said.

"Ah-ha," Gerry said at last, and then cleared his throat. Then he cleared it a few more times. "Well." He shrugged. "Hell with it. To each his own. To tell you the truth, my brother-in-law is gay, and I never thought it was much of a big deal. Congratulations. When's the big day?"

Hal lifted his wrist and checked his watch. "In about five hours. Unless they don't get my mother here on time."

"What the hell are you doing here, man, if you're getting married today?" Gerry demanded. He waved at the door. "Go on, go on!"

Hal rose, unhurried, and smiled. "It's not a very formal ceremony. But yes, I should probably get going."

"Where are you going for the honeymoon?" Gerry asked, rising to follow him to the door of the trailer.

"We're staying here," Hal said. "Morgan's not big on travel."

"Going to Disneyland, at least?"

Hal rubbed the side of his face and shuffled his feet. "No. We're just going to stay at home and have the honeymoon there."

He tried not to make it sound sexual, but knowing Morgan, it would be, and he was sure that echoed in his voice.

Probably because he was so looking forward to it.

"Ah," Gerry said and gave him a wink. He leaned forward and spoke sotto voce, even though they were the only ones in the small office. "Between you and me, I heard the guys talking about some new sex club not far from here. Supposed to be all chic but not some yuppie joint, either. I'd check it out if I didn't think the wife would kill me if she found out."

Hal found it harder not to blush this time. "Ah," was all he said, and hoped Gerry would leave it at that.

But Gerry was looking at a blank wall, and Hal got the idea that some rather sordid scenes were playing across it, just for him. "They say people do it sometimes right there in front of you." He stared almost glassy-eyed at the wall for a moment, then blinked, and gave Hal a rueful grin. "Equal opportunity, too, if you get my drift. The guys were talking about some Asian guy who climbed on a table last night, and some big guy wearing nothing but a thong and an eye mask came up behind him and—well, the guys didn't elaborate, but I got the impression it was something else. Man, if I could catch a show where the one on the table was a *woman*...."

It had been something else, all right, Hal thought, and now it was he who stared at the wall, remembering. He could still see the smooth arch of Morgan's spine, could feel the curve of it beneath his fingers. He could smell the oil and musk as he bent down to his waist and slid his tongue down between Morgan's sweet and tender cheeks.

And the sounds. And after, when they'd gone back to his room, and Morgan had showed him, in private this time, what it felt like to be on the other end of the performance.

"Hal?"

Hal blinked, blushed crimson, and then cleared his throat. "Yes. Sorry."

Gerry laughed and slapped him on the shoulder. "Could be something to check out, eh? Now go on, get out of here and get married. I look forward to working with you when you get back. And I wasn't kidding about that design work. You and your partner want to work on some other projects, you just let me know."

"Will do," Hal said, nodded a good-bye, and left.

There hadn't been an earthquake, exactly, when Morgan had brought down the Oasis, but it had been as good as one, and it had totaled the entire infrastructure of the construction on the site. It worked out well, though, because it turned out that Eagan had bought it all in Morgan's name, and when Morgan saw the parking garages and office buildings and cookie-cutter condos, Hal knew he would have torn them down himself. They'd made up the new design together, and it didn't surprise Hal at all that the place ended up looking like a Japanese village plunked down in the middle of Santa Monica. Modernized, of course, but the bones were there, as were the cherry trees. There were a few botanicals that didn't want to grow there, but Shinju said not to worry, she'd talk them into it. Mostly the *kitsune* would be living there anyway.

And maybe, if everything went well, Hal's mother and Aunt Lottie.

HE SAW them standing at the edge of the empty lot that hid the Oasis as he came around the construction barrier. His face broke into a grin, and he double-timed it under the scaffolding, then gave up and ran as soon as he was clear, leaped over a pile of paving stones, and gathered his mother in his arms.

"Oh, Mom," he said when he was able. "Mom, I've missed you so much."

"It's good to see you, too, Howard," she said and hugged him tight. She pulled back from him and waved vaguely at the street. "The driver let us off here and took Shinju around to some other entrance. She said you would be by before too long, and so you were! We had a nice little chat here in the sunshine while we waited. Such a lovely place this will be when it's finished. It's a shame about this empty lot, though."

He kissed the top of her gray hair. "Mom, I'm so glad you came."

She slapped him lightly on the arm. "As if I would have missed your wedding!"

"Especially after carrying on about when it was going to happen for so long," Aunt Lottie said, and then she craned her neck toward the construction site. "So—where's this handsome fellow, Hallie?"

Hal nodded to the empty lot. "Just here."

They both looked at the empty lot and then looked back at Hal, uncertain.

"Shinju did explain it to you?" Hal said, hoping to God she had.

"She said that Morgan was a bit different," his mother said, using her polite voice.

"She said he was some sort of magical place, too, but we chalked that up to some sort of metaphor," Aunt Lottie added.

Hal sighed. "It's not a metaphor. But you'll understand that soon enough." He offered them each an arm. "Come on. I'll take you inside."

"But Howard," his mother protested, "this is just an empty—"

They stepped forward into the Oasis.

"—lot," she finished weakly. And held on tightly to his arm.

"What the hell is this?" Lottie demanded.

"This," Hal said, quietly, "is Morgan."

"He—" His mother blinked several times and then let out her breath in a rush. "He is beautiful."

And he was. The main building—the bar in the former incarnation of the Oasis—still needed a lot of work, but the grounds were already amazing. The lot was full of light and sun reflecting off the glass, and there were lots of plants and trees. There were all the Japanese varieties that Morgan had grown to please his mother and himself, but he'd dogged everyone until they'd brought him "a book of Kansas," and so there was also wheat and great oak trees and whole acres of lilies and irises. He'd heard Hal mention his mother liked lilacs, apparently, because right now there was an archway made of them, all the way from the street entrance to the garden where they would have the wedding.

The little club Gerry had found out about was in the back. Morgan had sworn he'd hide all trace of it, though, while Hal's mother was in town.

"It's breathtaking, Howard." She reached up to pluck a lilac, then stopped and quickly withdrew her hand, looking guilty.

Hal smiled and reached up and plucked it for her. "You're supposed to pick the flowers and the fruit," he explained gently. He nodded to the tree, where the plucked flower was already growing back. "See?"

His mother's eyes were very wide. "Goodness." Then she frowned again, eyeballing the bush with a strange criticism. "But—you are marrying a *shrub*?"

"No. Ah—" Hal ran his hand through his hair and then glanced upwards. "Morgan, if you have a minute?"

And then, as if he had always been standing there, Morgan stood beneath the lilac arch. He was wearing, for some reason, a pair of dark jeans and a plaid button-down shirt, a huge belt buckle that read RODEO CHAMPION, and cowboy boots—with fringe.

The Kansas book, Hal thought, with a sigh.

Morgan was smiling, but he was clearly nervous. "Yes, Howard?"

Hal took his arm, smiled, and turned back to his mother. "Mom? *This* is Morgan. In addition to the garden and the lilacs."

Morgan reached out and took her hand, smiling like the sun. "Mrs. Porter. It's such a pleasure to meet you." He glanced up at the lilacs. "Did you like the flowers?"

"Oh, yes," she said. "Thank you."

Hal could see the questions rolling around in his mother's mind. Funny, though, how the fact that Morgan was male didn't faze her at all. And she was working very hard on the "he's a magical place" thing too. He wondered, for the thousandth time in the past few weeks, why he had ever doubted that she would accept and love him no matter what.

Shinju appeared, too, though she came the more traditional way by walking up a flagstone path. She was wearing gold today, which from what Hal understood of *kitsune* lore, was because of the wedding.

"I apologize for leaving you so quickly once we arrived, but I knew Hal would want a moment with you first, and I needed to discipline a new servant. And change. Goodness, but traveling is a dusty business." She smiled at Hal's mother. "How do you find my son?"

Hal saw that his mother's eyes fixated a bit too long on Shinju's magic arm, but she said nothing of that and only returned her smile. "He's absolutely beautiful, of course." She turned to Morgan, who was beaming, and then made a "oh, to heck with it" motion with her hand and drew him into a slightly awkward hug. "Welcome to the family, Morgan."

When they parted, Shinju came up and took her hand. "Come, Beverly. I have arranged for us to have a small tea together before the ceremony begins. And we'll get you settled in your rooms. My man will see to the pressing of your dresses, and I've enchanted him so that he will appear to provide you whatever you require. I hope you don't feel that was too forward?"

"Oh," Hal heard his mother say, sounding a little overwhelmed. "That's just fine. Thank you."

"You keep slaves?" Lottie asked, a little suspicious.

"Just the one," Shinju said airily. "But don't worry. It's the way his species functions, you see—they *must* be enslaved, or they can't live, bless their souls. This one is having trouble adjusting, but he's beginning to understand how I expect him to behave, and now that he has his boundaries, he's settling in just fine. And one day, with the proper tutelage, he might learn to live without having so much of himself wrapped up in others. But we won't rush his education. And he's so cute and round. Like a little Buddha but with bigger ears. Quite a bit bigger."

"Sure," Lottie said, looking a little uncertain, but she shrugged and returned to examining her surroundings, nodding approvingly as she craned her neck around the Oasis again. "Bev, I think you should reconsider refusing to move out here if this is where you'd get to live."

"I would like to urge you to reconsider also," Shinju was saying. "At tea I will show you Hal and Morgan's plans for the new housing. If you would like to have your own domain altered to suit your tastes, this would of course be no problem at all."

Hal and Morgan stood side by side, watching them disappear down the path.

"How long, do you think, before she convinces them?" Morgan asked after a while.

"They might last an hour," Hal conceded, grinning. Then he laughed, grabbed Morgan by the waist, and spun him around.

"I'm so excited, Howard!" Morgan said, after Hal had put him back down and finished kissing him. "I can't wait to show you my costume for the ceremony." He nudged him gently in the belly. "And what are *you* wearing?"

Hal tensed, just a little. "Ah, just a tuxedo. It's sort of traditional where I come from. Is that okay?"

Morgan beamed and tugged at his belt buckle. "Like this?"

"A bit fancier," Hal admitted.

"I'm sure it will be beautiful, whatever it is." Morgan hugged him again. "Oh, Howard. I'm so happy. I never dreamed I could be this happy."

Hal hugged him back. *Me too.* He looked out across the edge of the Oasis, catching the shadow of what he had started thinking of as the World Beyond. He thought of the construction site and the bus stop and the day he had stood there and seen the Oasis for the first time.

"Do you ever wonder," Hal said, "how I ended up here? I mean—how did I see you? Your mother swears she didn't cast any spell, not that first time. She says I simply looked over and saw you. Just like that." He shook his head. "I just can't figure out how it happened."

He expected Morgan to say something cute or trite about fate, but he paused for a moment instead to think about it, and when he spoke, he asked, "What were you thinking about, Howard, when you looked at me that first time?"

"Thinking?" Hal repeated. He frowned and stared off into the air, trying to remember. "It had been a long day, I remember that. I was hot and tired." He thought a little harder. "Lonely," he said quietly. "I was lonely. I stared off at the empty lot and wished, just for a moment, that I had somebody to go home to, to look forward to seeing, so I wouldn't be so lonely."

"Ah," Morgan said, very softly, and then let his head fall down against Hal's shoulder. "Well, there's a very strong likelihood that, at that moment, I was looking out at the world and thinking much the same thing. Except, obviously, I was wishing that the somebody would come to me."

"So," Hal said, a strange, butterfly feeling dancing in his chest. "No magic, then."

"Oh no," Morgan said, his voice full of light and love. "Absolutely, there was magic." He kissed Hal on the cheek. "I need to go prepare. See you soon?"

Hal kissed him back again. "Very soon."

He watched Morgan fade away and then stood there a few moments, letting his thoughts and feelings, hopes and dreams, and pretty much everything roll around in his head. He wondered what his life would be like now. He wondered what it would be like to live practically forever. He wondered if his mother would choose to live that long with him. He wondered, giving himself a little cross across his chest just to be respectful, how much of this magic had been the Holy Mother's doing.

He smiled. He suspected, privately, that it was quite a lot.

He reached up, stroked one of the lilacs in an almost sensual caress, and headed back into the main building to try and hunt down his tux.

IT WAS a bright, sunny afternoon in the city of Santa Monica, California, and everyone was out walking and enjoying the weather. For reasons none of them could name, a lot of people found themselves wandering down to the construction site on the south end of town, and after they stood there awhile, some of them felt compelled to walk out into the center of the empty lot, which, despite being nothing but sand and weeds, suddenly seemed like the most inviting place in the world.

Some of them said they saw a man. Many of them said they saw a man, actually, but they argued over what they saw, exactly. One group seemed to see a well-built, sandy-haired man in a very nice but plain black tuxedo, and they said that he looked a little uncomfortable in it, though they also allowed that he looked very happy. Still others said they saw a slight, very beautiful Asian man with long, flowing hair wearing some sort of golden robe or gown— but there was a lot of argument here, too, because some people saw trees printed on the gown, and some saw cherry blossoms, and some swore to God they saw a whole wheat field. Some say that when he moved, they saw him burn bright as the sun.

Some people said they saw both men, and then they nudged and winked at their neighbors and added, "And they were having one hell of a kiss too."

Everyone agreed that they had seen a truly bizarre number of foxes, and that for some reason, most of them seemed to have more than one tail.

But the part that they remember, the part that people still talk about, is that once the rumors of the two men and all the foxes died down, they heard soft, beautiful music, a lot of laughter, and then the bright, cloudless blue sky began to send down rain. Not a torrent, just a soft, gentle shower, and because it was glistening in the sun, it looked like sheets of diamonds were falling down on that empty lot in the middle of the construction site. The people laughed and smiled and twirled in the rain and gasped in wonder as countless rainbows arced across the sky.

And on their way back home, the elderly Japanese couple quietly agreed that it was absolutely the most beautiful *kitsune* wedding they'd ever seen.

HEIDI CULLINAN has always loved a good love story, provided it has a happy ending. She enjoys writing across many genres but loves above all to write happy, romantic endings for LGBT characters because there just aren't enough of those stories out there. When Heidi isn't writing, she enjoys cooking, reading, knitting, listening to music, and watching television with her family. Heidi also volunteers frequently for her state's LGBT rights group, One Iowa, and is proud to be from the first Midwestern state to legalize same-sex marriage.

Visit Heidi's web site at http://www.heidicullinan.com and her blog at http://amazoniowan.livejournal.com/.

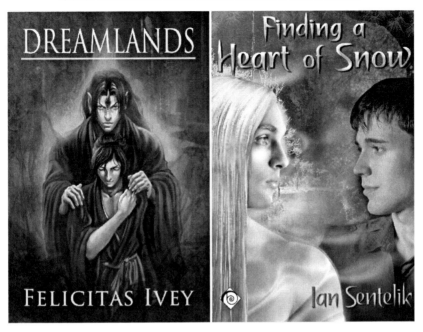
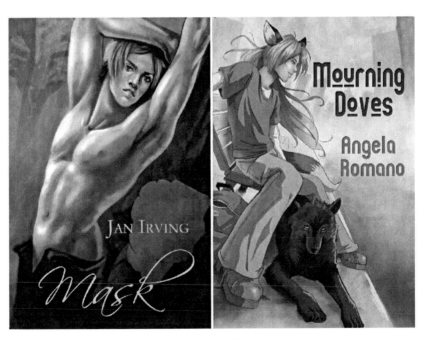

Lightning Source UK Ltd.
Milton Keynes UK
23 February 2010

150514UK00002B/63/P